D1167397

HOW TO BE MEDIOCRE

J.D DIPALMA

RED
PENGUIN
Books

Thank you to all who have given this book—and myself—a chance. Thanks especially to my parents, Don & Hannah, Ryder & Noeks, and the ER staff. I love you all dearly.

Please be sure to listen to the soundtrack for the book by JD Dipalma as well. Songs including "It's All Over," "No Pressure," "Oh Brother," and "Long Long Gone."
To hear all the music, all of it and more are available on Spotify and Apple Music

"Long Long Gone" is dedicated to my good friend Stevenson. Love and miss you, bud.

Contents

ONE

Meet Doug, The Loser

So I head down to the basement as I've done God knows how many times before. I duck under the low hanging part of the ceiling, the one disadvantage to being six-foot-two. I flick the amp on and wait for it to warm up. I walk over to the guitar rack, consisting of five guitars I overpaid for and treat like crap. I've got three electrics and two acoustics. An Epiphone Les Paul, a Mexican Fender Strat, an Ibanez hollow body, a Martin DRS1, and a Guild acoustic from '75 that was a gift from an ex-fiancee's mom; the deal was I keep the guitar, she keeps the big T.V. I know the Epiphone needs to be re-strung so I break out a pack of Ernie Ball 12-gauge electric strings. I love a full sound over a thin one. Typical punk rock. I imagine this is how hunters feel cleaning their guns as they need to every so often, just getting in the mindset of what to expect when they get out there. I start taking the old strings off and putting the new ones on. I tighten the top three strings, turning the pegs away from me, and tighten the bottom three towards me. The tuner's battery is low so I go over to the piano to tune. The only bummer is I have to run upstairs and turn the lights on. The only way to turn the piano on is to flip the switch; God only knows how many other people have those kinds of outlets in their place. I hit E2, A2, D3, G3, B4 and E4 all to the sounds of the dehumidifier in the background. I plug in and de-tune the top E string to drop D.

My pad and paper is right where I left it the day before, and the ideas start flowing. Time to write a hit song that most likely will go nowhere, and I will be the only one who hears it. I'm good—but not quite up to par with what's marketable. I'm not where I need to be with my social media presence so they're going another way—a feeling I know every average-joe musician can relate to. I just want one good show, one good EP, and one good swoop of recognition for something I've worked hard for and won't see the recognition.

This process has gone on every other day from the time I was 11 until now at 26 years old. I know I have to grow up—and I have, to a certain extent. The fiancee' and I didn't work for many reasons. I was always trying to be creative and she just couldn't see why I try so hard for something that'll never love me back. She gave me all the love I could want, but it wasn't the love I wanted. I wanted attention and I see that now. I don't regret ending things with her, God knows she spent all her time and effort on material things, too. Hers were shoes, booze and dudes with washboard stomachs; apparently, dad bods are only cool if you're a dad.

I have a full-time job at a school for disabled children as a teaching assistant, and I'm almost done with my degree in early childhood education. So I'm well aware that being a rockstar is well in the past, but fuck, it would be so cool. The girls, the house, the money—who knows what I could have been if I had gotten lucky and played that show that one time, or met with that agent who was a little skeevy. All the things you hear about having to sacrifice everything about yourself and your morals for the entertainment business seem to be all too true. There doesn't seem like a whole lot of room for real art unless you're a trendsetter, and I know damn skippy I'm not one.

I love every type of music you can throw at me. Punk, Rock, Alternative, Jazz, Hip-Hop, Country, R&B, Soul, Blues, on and on it goes. There's no genre I dislike, but certain artists I can do without; no shit-talking here. Every song is someone's art and a pure expression of what they may be going through or what they need to say, even if it is about drugs, ass or their pickup truck. I'm no different. I've written about girls, anti-government protest, medical conditions, all while silently ripping off the Beatles like everyone else.

I finish the "session," if you can call it that, and walk upstairs to be greeted by a wet-nosed creature by the name of Bruce, the family dog. He's a standard poodle who thinks the world of me and my crumbs. He follows me into the kitchen where Mom has made dinner. Living with your parents at this age really isn't that bad, but you can't help but feel a tiny bit of shame when all your buddies went away to school and you're still asking her the same question for fifteen years: "How'd that sound, Mom?"

"Sounded good, hon!" She's always been the support system I need. She lets me do what I love while making sure I don't fall behind and end up a loser. I've come pretty close a few times, but she knows when I go too far. Spending a month's paycheck on a new amplifier is all well and fun while living under Mom's roof, but she made it clear each time with her usual jingle: "Doug, you know you can't be spending money like that when you're on your own." There are days when I think Freud would tie me to a couch and make me ramble until I'm blue in the mouth.

She plops down the usual Wednesday dinner: spaghetti bolognese with garlic bread. We chat about our respective days while Bruce damn near plops his head in my lap. Say what you want about the little scrounger, but his sense of timing is better than most rhythm guitar players. As I finish rattling on about the latest Blink 182 record, because Matt Skiba is a legend (piss off if you think otherwise) Dad pops in from a long day at work. You want to talk about honor and conviction, talk to him for ten minutes and be prepared to be humbled. Dad was a drummer in a wedding band back in the day and has always been my coach and critic. The words "that riff sucks more than a taj massage parlor," will echo in my brain forever. Nobody gets anywhere without responding to criticism. Say what you will about music critics or people on any social media, but to me, the best work comes from the knee jerk reaction of "fuck you, I'll prove you wrong."

Dad always seems to know what I'm up to musically. He knows all my really great days through to my taj massage days. I feel like artists can sense when you lie through your teeth about how things are going. Being full of shit is a given when dealing with people like me. You have to play the game of "I'm the next best thing," and after a while, it's incredibly tiresome. I've quite had it, to be honest, hence why I'm shutting down operations on being the next KISS, Ramones, Toby Keith, Zach de LaRocha, or whatever phase I'm into that week. Putting on a happy face while internally screaming takes a toll on you.

"Sorry, hon, it was all hands today. Four hours overtime, though, so progress." The fact that the man can work four hours overtime doing engineering at a hospital and I can't even man up to going in on a holiday to help when grading falls behind says volumes about the differences in our work ethics. Maybe it's because he has a wife, house and a kid at home to feed, and had it all by the time he was my age, but it's things like this that snap me back to reality. There is no real substitution for hard work and it took me a while to learn that.

Mom gives him a big hug while he gives her a pinch on her backside, as I throw up in my mouth a little and die on the inside. I ignore it and ask him about his day. "Had to fix the AC in the ER and co-ordinate where the cement truck will go tomorrow to fix the sidewalk, so a pretty standard day. How about you, big man?" he asks, almost as though I'm still seven years old to him. Then again my mentality isn't that far off. "Just went to work, came home and played a little while," I reply, rotating my fork full of spaghetti into a spoon like I saw my grandfather do once.

"How'd work go? Anything on an open position?"

"Dad I still got a semester left to go. I sort of have to be certified to be a teacher to get a job as one."

"You have to market yourself now while you're a possibility. What's the point in putting in all that effort if you're not going to make them recognize it when the time comes?" I truly hate it when he's right, which is often.

I finish up dinner, do some studying and then lie down in bed. I start jotting down some lyric ideas on the notes app on my phone when Dad pops in.

"Hey, you awake, bud?"

"Yeah, what's up?"

He turns my light on and sits on the edge of my bed. All that's missing is a glass of chocolate milk and footy-pajamas and we've got my "birds and bees" talk all over again. Spoiler alert, both experiences have an equal amount of tears.

"So I was thinking about when you get a job and everything. I know this is going to sound harsh but I'd like you to move out when you save enough for rent on an apartment and make it on your own."

I couldn't help but drop my jaw. "You're kicking me out?" He looks at me as though I wasn't listening at all.

"You heard what I said. When you get a job and start making real money."

"Dad what about all my equipment? I can't take all that to an apartment."

He takes a deep breath and states the words I was hoping would never come. "Well you can keep a lot of it here still but maybe you can sell some of it and—" I don't even hear the rest because it's not an option. I say without thinking about it, "What the fuck? No way—I use all of that stuff."

"Tell me one time in the past three years when you used that sound system at a live show Tell me when you used that recording software, or even when the last live show you played even was."

I know the answer of course; five years ago at a block party that went down like a Led Zeppelin. Spoiler alert, that's how they (Led Zepplin) got their name. Inspired by Keith Moon, no less.

"Why are you doing this to me?" He says as calmly as he can while clenching a frustrated fist.

"It's time to grow up. You have tried this for long enough. Obviously, music is as important to you as it is to me. I'm not saying get rid of the guitars or pianos, but the stuff you don't use can go on to someone else who could get more use out of them since you're not. I wouldn't be doing my job as a father if I let you continue this same delusion of fame that I had. You're a dreamer, but someone has to keep you tethered."

The lump in my throat grows until my larynx peels. I am so upset.

"Think about it. Please. I'm sorry to do this but it's time."

I know it's time, but it's not even on my terms. It's not even terms I agree with. I know in my heart of hearts that he is right, but as I said; sometimes you get that drive of "Fuck you, I'll show you I can do it." And my motivation changes from "Alright, it's time" to "Here we go again."

TWO

A Day in the Life

S o I wake up the next day feeling fresh as an open bag of manure. I'm pretty sure being hit with a shovel is far more pleasing than your support system giving up on you. But this is how it is. Even if I had made it, sometimes a record label will not have faith in the work you do. Sometimes you have to crack your fingers, look yourself in the mirror and say, "It's go time." I'm pretty sure if all those action heroes can do it, I can too. When I get home, I'm going to figure out a kick-ass song and prove to everyone I'm not a loser. But until then, I've got work and then attend the school my parents have paid for like a blessing: who am I kidding here? It's not going to happen.

That, quite literally, is how most of my mornings are. A hot cup of optimism to be spiked with a shot of steaming reality. Look at it sitting there like vegetable oil on top of water highlighting differences in density. Speaking of which, that's what my preceptor is showing my class today. I take a shower and sift through the checklist in my head on what I have for today. I don't know why I think about it in the shower since it feels like two different types of drowning. And of course, Bruce is there licking my leg to try and get some water. I get out and fill the bowl for the silly creature. Man, some days I wish I had it as easy as he does. All he has to remember is where to poop and which couch not to jump on after Mom cleans it. All greeted with a nice belly rub and treat. Lucky little twerp.

I get dressed in my usual sweater vest and khakis. The kids usually get upset if I don't wear my vest. It's become my thing, although, I did try the whole Angus Young getup with an inflatable SG to walk around with for Halloween. It was all fun and games until I bent to get a pencil and ripped a hole exposing my butt crack. I almost was seen, but I walked horizontally to the bathroom with a pin to close the back end of the shorts. I could have been forced to stay at least 500 feet away from the school if I had been caught.

My car isn't too much a dumpster pile, but a 2004 Jeep Wrangler sure knows how to fall apart if it knows how to do anything at all. Girls sure do love a lift kit with the doors off in the summer, though. The commute to school is only about 20 minutes but I make it about 30, waiting in line for coffee. Molding America's youth is tiring work, especially with the shit pay that TA's get. I can't wait for that pay bump when I graduate.

Cut to my dumb ass spilling coffee all over me while putting a bit of sugar in. So now I look like I used to look in third grade with a water fountain, or if you want to get to the pathetic part, last summer at the Honolulu beach party for the staff. Although to be fair, in third grade it wasn't either my fault or real.

I run into the bathroom to try and dry it off for a split second but it never seems to really help. Guess I'll be walking around all day with my jacket in the front and tied around my waist like a kid on 90s Nickelodeon, huh?

It's scenarios like this that make me come back to Earth and send my delusion of fame and fortune down with it. I can't even keep coffee together so how am I supposed to play the Garden with a stain on my pants? I ought to stamp "Loser" on a couple of different angles of my head so that I'm covered 360 degrees. But then I get in the car and a killer song comes on the radio and I fly full speed to work with all green lights and get a good parking spot so I feel all ten kinds of awesome. If you think the sudden ups and downs are a little concerning, I've noticed them as well. The truth is, the feeling of trying to make it in this world comes and goes this often. To be able to stay positive, and know that I have made a positive impact with music is all I want. Any observer of my situation can point out that I already make a contribution and impact by helping kids, and they're right. I do. But the impact with music is something I just want a little notoriety for. If not the world, just a little respect on my scene. I live on Long Island in New York. It has God knows how many bars, but the venues you want to play are well known: The Last Exit Club, Point Ollie's Bar and Grill, and even some of the coffee houses like Milk and Sugar. Those are the spots most bands play. The crowds are either really vocal or talk shit behind your back. So if you suck, you'll know it, but in the worst ways. The kicker here is, I've been told I'm really good and should keep going. But the agonizing disappointment is just becoming too much to handle. I love writing music and I don't know if writing is something I can stop doing. Give me a little time and I can figure out where you want the song to go and how to make it appealing. But lately every time I get up on stage I realize, "Fuck, I'm going to be here a while." Doing things for me is really not how making it works. To really "make it," you have to love performing and singing things to which you had little-to-no contribution in their creation—unless you really are the best of the best with writing. I know I have talent, but I'm not good enough. It's like I want to perform, but have no interest in what a ghostwriter wants. It sure would be great if I could put as much knowledge and effort as I do with music and art into work, though.

There is nothing quite like that morning wake up and hearing your first class roar with morning hormones while you open the door. God, I hate middle schoolers, but the kid I sit with is pretty awesome. Bobby has autism but is far smarter than me or anyone my age. He just has a hard time with his behavior and staying focused. So I sit next to him and practically point my finger on his paper and say "focus."

After about six-and-a-half hours of paper tapping, I run home and shower before going out to school, although I can't help but notice something peculiar about my car. You see, I never drive a car with a tire that's flat. It's so bizarre. It's like I grabbed the wrong tire for my car today—just threw it on by accident while leaving the house.

Sarcasm has become the best coping mechanism for frustration. Beats throwing a fit and jumping up and down like a pissed-off student when we commandeer a vape pen. I have no fathomable understanding of why kids use these things.

They don't have enough problems in life to know about smoking in order to de-stress. I used to be a pack-a-day smoker until it killed my singing voice—like I'll need it in the future, anyway.

I zip through traffic and hop in the shower to be greeted by a particular poodle. I lay low for a little while, then grab some food. I hate cooking for myself. It makes me feel self-sufficient. No, I'm not that totally useless, just lazy. I grab some food from the nearest fast food joint while dripping their special sauce down onto my beard and driving with one hand. Nobody can drive and eat quite like me. I've got it down to a science. I plop the fries and drink in the cup holder while...wait, why am I telling you? Piss off, it's my secret.

I whip into the parking lot then jolt into the building all the while crying on the inside at the stomach cramp I have from eating fried food too fast and then running. I'm quite the slob and dope, I'm well aware.

So now you've seen what my normal day consists of. Pretty bland, isn't it? Well, it was all pretty bland until this happens.

I turned a corner and out of nowhere I felt something nail me in the back of my head and I crash to the ground. "Oh my God, I'm so sorry!" a total babe yells as she jumps down the steps two at a time. "No worries. I'm okay," I say while pushing my sweatshirt to my head to stop the bleeding. She holds the sweatshirt for me while I rest on the wall and says "Did it hurt?"

Do any of you ever have an inner monologue? Of course not; you're normal people. My inner monologue is using the

Carlin 7 dirty words in various sentences that could scare away anyone, but I have to play it cool, you know?

"A little bit, but it shouldn't be too bad. Are you okay?"

"Yeah I was just...you're going to laugh at me," she says thinking twice about it.

"Try me."

"Well the new Slipknot just came out and I've been air drumming the blast beats all day. So it just slipped out of my hand and..."

Ladies and gentlemen if you think I stopped listening because of a severe head injury, you're only partly right. The fact that this woman listens to Slipknot, all the while knowing what a blast beat is, ordinarily makes my heart pump enough blood to keep all systems going. However, in this case, it's rushing to my forehead to clot the wound. I didn't even give a shit I was now late to a class that I'm only allowed two absences for. For a girl like this, whom destiny reaches out and chucks literature at you for, you stop and pay attention.

I look at her in sweet sincerity and utter, "To be fair, Weinberg does an outstanding job and nailed the last album." She looked at me as though I just uttered the secret phrase to her heart. This felt right. Keep in mind, I was engaged to be married, and I wasn't this optimistic in the entirety of our relationship. It's almost like that book to the head just dropped a shitty four-year relationship out and dropped in the most euphoric 70 seconds of my life.

"You like other types of music?" she inquires.

"Oh yeah" I reply in an understatement. "Primary thing I

spend my income on. It's what I wake up in the morning for." She bites her lip in a way that makes her seem a bit turned on. Hell, I'm down. She then said, "I was supposed to go to this concert on Friday but my friend didn't buy me a ticket so I can't go now." Anyone else spy an opening to flirt? Oh, I do. I say with as much cool as I can muster, "So that means you're free on Friday for dinner then?" I've never seen anyone blush this hard. Nailed it.

THREE

The Rolodex of Girls

She finishes blushing, I get her number, and then run off to class. Turns out her name is Angela. And I can't remember anything about the class I was taking because all I can think about is how Angela made me feel like I had been seen for the first time in my life. Obviously, I've been noticed and observed my whole life, but she really made me feel seen. In the brief time we saw each other, we had an unspoken connection and both agreed that we're into each other.

I bail out of class, get to my car, pull out of the parking lot and drive home. I start to have the usual bout of anxiety I usually have at night time. The kind you usually have laying in bed thinking the world is about to crash down all because you did something stupid years ago. There's tea time in London, smoke breaks for health care workers, and anxiety time for me. Can't help it, it's in my family history and it'll only get passed on to the next in line.

I can't help but think, "What if this girl sees the real me? The real loser that lies just below the surface of the usual mediocrity I have?" I honestly think this is why I perform and write music. I can't feel my own happiness so I get on stage and act the fool to make people like me. Isn't that pathetic? I know I'm not alone, other performers feel similar, but there are times where I can't help but feel I'm alone; just this overwhelming feeling of the whole world shrinking down to the size of my silhouette and applying enough pressure to make me crack and spill. This girl and I exchanged maybe five sentences before I ran off to class, but what if in those five sentences she could see I'm full of shit? I'm a performer, therefore a liar. A lot of the things I say or do are just carbon copies and ideas I have seen before; I re-structured them and made them my own. Do you know how many times E—B—C#m —A chords have been used over with new words? Ask any musician, they'll tell you.

This cackle of nonsense is what goes on in my head at any given time. Something positive or negative can happen, I'll still be rambling. But in all seriousness, my collective dating history is not New Year's highlight reel of the progress I've made and great events that have taken place. It looks more like an in memoriam or old DVDs of hockey's best fights. And that doesn't just apply to women, but the riffs I've written, the script ideas I've jotted down, or the aspirational dreams that get anchored down by life and time. So let's see the "who's who" of Doug's greatest hits, including cameos from one night stands and fuck buddies, you never know who'll pop in—or out.

So let's start with the obvious, the ex-fiancee'. Catherine and I met online and if not for that we never would have met. She was working finishing up college and taking her final teaching exams, while here I was...not. For the lack of better wording, I was more or less a fish on an unlit barbecue; I was about to be burnt. I had all this stuff going with music deals I was so underprepared for. When we started going out I was about to sign a contract with a foreign record company. Her dad was a lawyer who said: "Bullshit, let me read it." Thank Christ he did because I was about to sign a 360 deal—a deal that takes money from every aspect of revenue including live shows and merchandise, which is ordinarily where musicians make most of their money. I bowed out and was swimming in familiar waters again. She really took care of my dumb ass while I couldn't have cared less about myself or what happened to me. I did tell her though I would be a stay-at-home husband if it came down to the idea of having children and forming a future. But the more she'd tell me about her school assignments, the more I became fascinated by it. I told her about writing music and said that if she ever needed help with an assignment, I'd help. Kind of like telling a lawyer that you've read Cat in the Hat and going "Yeah, I can read all good like!"

But the more I read up on her books and papers, the more I knew I should go into this myself. I got it so much easier than I got into music. It felt like it was written for me. I'm a firm believer that if something is coming naturally to you, you should dive deep with it. It could be the answer or droid you're looking for.

But I still had this pinging in the back of my mind about music. I wasn't ready to give it up yet. I would go to school part-time and be writing constantly. I believed in myself even if nobody else did. But I was still getting my school work done and passing everything with top marks, so nobody could say shit to me. The more classroom time I did the more I realized that this was my niche, but I realized this wasn't the atmosphere I wanted to come home to. I wanted to come home and be with a wife and enjoy "playtime." Yes hanky-panky, but I wanted to travel and act like a kid when I didn't have this looming sense of responsibility—to be selfish and not have to care about anyone else when I finished work. And when you have kids, you can't be so selfish. So I dropped that bomb on her and the next day there was an engagement ring on my bedside table. I thought that I'd have been crying like a baby, but I sat there, exhaled and went back to sleep.

I know it sounded shallow and hollow to not show more emotions, but what can you do when you know this is the right decision for two of you? You just have to accept that though you may love each other, it doesn't mean that you're right for each other. Heavy shit, right? Not all pussy and music jokes up in here.

Before Catherine and the two other lovely ladies you'll meet —that's right, two more—let's talk about Winnie. Winnie is a lovely young lady who I met while cheating on my high school girlfriend. What a catch I am, huh?

Winnie and I met in person, which is odd enough for this day and age. During my first attempt at college, at the time I went for nursing but dropped it because of catheters—well, yuck. That's the joke version. I left because I was atrocious at the topic and I didn't feel like wasting time on something I knew I couldn't do. I digress: I was on academic probation with Winnie and we hit it off with a reference I made from a movie she saw. We exchanged numbers since the counselor advised us to—therefore he's to blame. But when the flirting started I quickly advised her I had a girlfriend. However, that didn't seem to stop her (or me) from exchanging dirty texts. And although this behavior was beyond revolting, I have to say I was having quite fun with a girlfriend and a dirty secret. The girlfriend and I ended without speaking of Winnie but I'm sure she must have known. She was not a dumb girl and you can only say "I'm sleeping over at my classmate's house" so many times while explaining that Winnie is a guy's name, too.

Not even a week after that relationship ended, I set up a proper date with Winnie. And I have to say after the facade dropped and we were two single people, it was an absolute mismatch. There was a true sense that we should just be friends—naked friends at best. However, she couldn't see it. She really loved me and wanted to be my girlfriend. I realized I needed time to grow, to mature, and become a better person, but she was not having it. It got rather crazy the way she would retaliate against me. What started with pictures of her with other guys to make me jealous turned into trips to my job to see me.

You have to be careful with what you set onto the world through your emotions or your genitals. I wish I hadn't hurt her. I really do. I feel that in a way I could've loved her more than just as a friend, but the people we became when we were around each other was just not who we really were. I set out to get a jump on my attempt at a music career and she went into a five-year relationship and found the love of her life. A messy beginning turned out to be a great ending, for one of us, anyway.

It's like life takes one turn and—fucking hell! Did you see that? That squirrel popped out of nowhere, man. I swear to

God they are the ballsiest animals to run across the street. It's like that scene in "Watership Down" when that bunny wasn't expecting anyone to pop out on the road and then . . . sorry! I have become distracted by the girls. Last time, I promise. Although, this is the one with the two girls. I have to tell this one in the car before I go in.

So I started working really hard when it came to honing my craft as a songwriter and performer. For five solid years, I was really killing it. Growing and maturing along the way. I stayed single for five years to make sure that when I met someone I was ready. And then there was this one show when I was knocking the crowd dead. I actually sold the place out. The first and last time it ever happened for me. No album or EP, either. All of it was word of mouth and the occasional fan posting my set on a social media platform. I was hanging backstage and someone actually asked me to sign a flyer. My first autograph! I couldn't believe it. She was a real stunner too, so I was sure someone had sent her back as a joke, but it was real. She even asked me to dinner in this nervous way, as though I was almost unobtainable. She said "Ummm, if it's not too much to ask, can I, like, I don't know, ask you to dinner sometime or like...no it's so stupid. I'm sorry." I was stunned saying, "Can you? Please, this never happens to me."

Let me tell you all something. Artists are people, too. They have families they have hopes and dreams, but they aren't above anyone. We're all the same in the way of hierarchy. No matter what anyone says, we're all the same degree of scum, and I say that in the nicest and most sarcastic tone.

Anyway, we exchanged numbers and Grace took me out. It was nice, very romantic and very quaint. But even sitting down getting to know her I could tell I was not ready for commitment. We walked to the car and she asked me out again; I told her, "This is all very sweet and kind of you, but I have to tell you I'm not looking for anything serious. The best I can do right now is be casual with no expectations, but I doubt you're interested in that."

To my surprise, she said, "Actually, I was thinking the same thing." So we would hang out whenever we had the time for each other. She had her own place so it was always there where we'd have nights in, nights out, or nights in the bedroom. Those were becoming far more common than anything else, however. Those nights in the bedroom became lunches in bed, then those lunches became "I have 30 minutes before my next set. Want to get a quick one in?" We both agreed that even having a casual commitment to each other was a little more than we could handle so we agreed to be friends with benefits. And we were great friends with each other in the meantime. I'd drive her to doctors' appointments, she'd be there for me at shows when I was nervous, and we couldn't believe how great it was going. Then, a monkey wrench was thrown in.

A similar scenario happened with a girl named Alyssa. The difference was, she wanted something more serious with meaning. Though I was skeptical at first, we went out. And we fitted together like a puzzle. She was my other half for that time. She knew about Grace but was okay with it until we became monogamous. While on a date I mentioned to her, "You guys would probably get along well."

She chuckled and said, "We should probably get together without you and make you jealous."

I said in an entirely joking manner, "Threesomes are on the table then?"

And she didn't laugh but said in all seriousness, "I've always wanted to try it, so why not?" Without a second to lose, I texted Grace the pitch for one and somehow she agreed.

The number of times I said to myself "Holy shit, this is happening," can't be measured. I was bouncing off the walls for the date we had arranged. But alas, reality came crashing in. I don't know how open relationships or swingers do it because, in my experience, three-ways never end well. Someone just gets hurt.

The closer and closer the day came we'd all be texting each other in a group chat to define our limits and boundaries. The more they started chatting, the more they started to get to know and like each other as people. However, Alyssa couldn't help but notice I wasn't coming to my end of the bargain of committing to her. I wasn't changing my ways in the ways I had promised. And the inevitable question came up, "What does she give you that I don't?" And it's not that Grace did anything different or better, it's just I was set in my ways of being a free man and though I thought I could drop my fucking around, my actions were showing that I had no intentions of slowing down and being monogamous. So after she came into my car and saw Grace's sweatshirt in the back seat, it came crashing down on her that a future with me was not a possibility. In the next few days, Grace found a new man to whom she wanted to be faithful. I went from having the best possible arrangement there was, to having nothing.

The number of times I went to my basement to write while I was depressed couldn't be counted. And this was not something I'd want to vent to Mom about, so I kept it to myself. Bottle after bottle was being purchased, shows weren't being played when I was booked for them, they stopped booking me altogether, and I was left with nothing to show for my work. The last five years of building my act were now awash.

As I park my car and walk inside and down to the basement again I look at all the holes in the wall I've punched, dents in the ceiling I have made from lifting my guitar too high, markings on the wall from carrying amplifiers and cases in at 03:00 AM and I have come to a sobering thought. The choices I made are the ones I have to live with.

I made the choices to dedicate time and effort to these girls and gave less than what they deserved. I should have been all in for them because they were all in for me. Can I say they were regrets? Maybe, but it would be unfair to the life I live now. If I want things to work with this girl I met, I have to put my own selfish crap aside and realize it's not all about me anymore. Relationships are partnerships. If you can't commit, don't start one.

And as I sit here and play my acoustic, I have to say that— hold on . . . this sounds really good. What if I try it like . . . yeah! Holy shit! I love the way this sounds.

The above passage is what most musicians think when they find a riff they love or a melody that makes them stop a lesson they learned or a composed thought, and then focus on finishing what they deem a "masterpiece." Spoiler alert: most aren't, but this one, you can say, has potential.

FOUR

First Date Doug

───────────────

Holy shit, I think I've done it. I really think I've done it. I've written a hundred good riffs before and said to myself, "This is the single when it comes out," all the while never releasing anything I've recorded. But honestly, I have goosebumps. "Dad! Come down here quick!" My parents have had infinite fucking patience with me, and this is probably where they use it the most. I can hear to this day the sound of Dad exhaling, getting up slowly, muttering "Fucking kid never gives me a break." Then slowly comes down the stairs.

"What now?"

"Dad, I swear to God I got something good." I adjust my tuning and get my tempo back, and I start going to town. Even he looks at me with these wide eyes and is floored by it. He doesn't say anything though. He just gets behind the kit and starts playing. I know he likes it when he jumps behind the kit. He does this thing that sounds okay, but not great.

"No, Dad, stick to the snare and go to the hi-hat on the pre-chorus."

"Want one or two pedals on the kick?"

"Just stick to the one. Keep it simple." We hammer it out and take our time. It's kind of weird how when two musicians know they have something good, they laugh. Dad was laughing like he had just watched "Life of Brian."

Oddly enough a lot of the big "hits" in music were written in only a couple minutes. Sometimes if an artist is taking a long time with something, it just isn't right. But if it flows out naturally, you know you have something great. Sammy Hagar wrote how "Rock Candy" was a last-minute song because Montrose needed one more good song. It was damn near written in only a couple of takes. "The Lumberjack Song" was written in only twenty minutes because Jones and Palin needed a "way out" of the homicidal barber sketch. Even McCartney said "Yesterday" came to him in a dream. He just didn't believe he had written it for about two weeks. Sometimes a song just comes to you. Inspiration doesn't have a schedule.

"Doug I don't know how you came up with this but I really like it. The first song I've really loved of yours in a good many years." That hit me like a truck, man. When the guy you admire most loves something you do, no amount of money or fame can come close to the amount of pride and contentment you feel.

"So what do I do with it? I know I'm out of the game but, man, this one is good." He sits on his drum throne pondering. He told me the other day it's time to grow up, and here we are right back in the thick of that bug we both can't seem to shake. Creative people can't shake it no matter what. Years can go by and one song can get you back into "edit mode." If the song is good, they'll say "Shit, I should have thought of that." If they don't like it, they'll go sift through every second going, "Who the fuck thought of this?

Dad stands up and says, "Call Tim and just get it on tape." Tim is my producer/engineer who handles everything musical I do. We must have recorded a good twenty-plus songs, but we released none of them because I'm so scared of the rejection.

"Did anything happen today that got you grooving or thinking?" I have a big shit-eating grin on and tell him about Angela.

"You guys been texting?"

I know I have forgotten to do something. "Not yet. It only happened a couple of hours ago." "Text her tomorrow. Don't seem so desperate."

"Yeah, that sounds good."

I think we all know I don't make good decisions, so of course, I text her when he leaves and goes upstairs. "Dad, I'm actually pretty nervous about texting her."

"Why?"

Like he doesn't already know. "I'm so lousy at giving my all to people and I want this to be right, so if she agrees to go out with me, what do I do, how do I do it, what do I say?"

He makes a "timeout" motion and says, "One step at a time.

I've never seen you so nervous, so when I tell you this, try to follow through with it, please?"

I put the guitar down so he knows he has my full attention.

"Take a look at yourself and figure out what you as a person like to do when you're alone. Or what you do when you're in a bad mood to make yourself feel happy. After you work that out, ask her to do that with you as your first date. Because you'll know you've found the one when you can take them along and still enjoy yourself because their company makes you enjoy it more. Because if they can do that, you'll never want to be alone again."

And there I was thinking to myself, "Fuck, I should have thought of that." Sorry, it's the writer in me. So Dad runs upstairs and I do as I said I was going to do. I send her a text that keeps things light. Not too much pressure, yet sweet. "Hey! Great to meet you today. Can't wait to see you soon!" Then I wait a good fifteen minutes for a response. Fifteen minutes seems like an eternity to a millennial. She sends back "Heyy! Great bumping into you, too! Sorry about your head again! :(" It's my personal belief that if someone you're into gives you more than one "y," they're into you, too. Obviously, it's not a fact, just my experience.

Though I'd love to chat back and forth with her all night, I have sleeping to do and I want to talk with her more in-depth when we go out. I text her back, "No worries! It's not every day you get hit in the head by a beautiful girl. I usually have to wait for a relationship for that and it's usually a frying pan."

"Oh my God, you must have brain damage because I am not

beautiful, but thank you. And I have a few pans so I'll practice my aim."

By the way, she is a stunning woman. She looks like one of those girls who was an emo kid in junior high that's into flower power now that she's an adult, but would also look at home at an emo night. I send back "Oh lucky me. Btw when are you free?"

"I'm free Friday night if you are"

"I am, and that sounds good to me. What would you like to do?" What she sends next kind of breaks my heart. Because this is like the fifteenth time I've heard this in my time of dating. "Umm, I've never actually been on a date so I don't quite know what to do. Up to you really."

Now I'm all for feminism and breaking the glass ceiling, but some things shouldn't totally go away, in my opinion. Good men shouldn't be a dying breed. Netflix and chilling is fine when you're in a relationship, but have some substance, you low-aspiring fucks. Have an imagination. So I send her this, "That really breaks my heart in a way. What do you like to do as your hobbies?"

"I just listen to music, watch TV, hang with my friends and go to school really."

I'm about to shoot this date right in the five-hole. "How about I take you into town, go to the record store, book store, then grab some dinner? Keep it low pressure and just have fun?"

She steals my heart by saying "make it a comic book store and I'm ready to rage." God, she's one of the good ones.

Now it turns out we only have that one day together on campus so we can't even meet up for stuff before or after class, because she's a nursing major, so she's a busy girl. And I was hit in the head with a sociology book. I'm just grateful it wasn't anatomy and physiology. I don't know about anyone else, but when I have plans at the end of the week I'm looking to speed up time just so I can get going. My God, I hate waiting for a good thing when I know it's coming around the corner. Today was my average day minus meeting Angela. But my week has been more or less the same. Work, lounge around, school, then go and play music. The only other thing I could do was obsess over this song. I have all the music written but no lyrics at all. I'm sure that'll come in time slowly but surely. But until then, you have to move on with your life.

Friday comes and I'm at the record store an hour early. I actually shop before I'm supposed to shop along with her. I get the really good stuff and hide it in my car. As I shut the door she pulls up; success.

She comes out of her car and I'm already convinced that a ring is all I need. We have texted intermittently all week and she is as beautiful on the inside as she is out. She gives me a hug and the best date of my life starts.

She stops hugging me and says, "Let's go. I've been looking forward to this all week." We walk inside. "So where do you want to start? I know you like Slipknot but—Angela? Where'd you…"

"I'm over here!" She yells from behind the stacks. She's flipping through the stacks like I wasn't even there. "I've been on this punk kick so I'm probably going to be here a while."

Starting at "A" she pulls out a record or two (Alkaline Trio and Anti Flag) and puts them on the side. Moving on down the line she grabs Circa Survive, Descendents, and I Am the Avalanche. All awesome bands I listen to often. She hops over to metal and picks up Avenged Sevenfold. Rap and hip-hop get a look through and I hear "already have a lot of these." I think I'm tearing up. Then I hit her with the question of all questions that don't involve dropping to one knee. If you had to pick three records that can sum up who you are, which would you pick and why? I get a thousand-yard stare. A look that almost says, "That's not possible."

"Hold these and I'll go look."

I'm sitting on these chairs at a listening station watching these records like they're a new diamond necklace. I'm contemplating my own three records because I know she's going to ask me for my choices. I know not many people in this day and age buy full-length albums or take the time to listen to them, but some can change an outlook on life in just one listen. I've always heard of a song changing someone's life, and it happens more than you think. One lyric or the way a progression is played has sometimes turned my world upside down. So I urge everyone to take a listen to a full album that one of your favorite songs is on. She comes back with her three picks. And man oh man are they good picks.

She whips out the "untitled album" from Blink 182. "I don't know anyone our age who didn't listen to 'I Miss You' and cry a little inside," she says. "This whole album, bottom to top, is outstanding. It just goes to show a change in direction in life is not a bad thing. It could be the best thing. You can be the same person and mature without losing your friends or fans."

She puts that aside and puts up "Good Apollo. I'm Burning Star IV, Volume I: From Fear Through the Eyes of Madness" by Coheed and Cambria. "There's always going to be songs about relationships, drugs and alcohol, even politics. But hell I never knew you could write a song about the graphic novel series you have. You never know where inspiration can come from or the story behind it. Have you read the books he wrote? Goddamn, that guy is talented. Honestly one of the most influential artists on my life." Then finally she pulls out the red herring of the three, but holy crap it's a good pull. She pulls out "The Low End Theory" from A Tribe Called Quest. "I grew up with jazz around the house so this will always hold a place in my heart. It couldn't be more on point than in the opening song 'Excursions.' You can find the abstract listening to hip-hop. My pops used to say it reminded him of be-bop. You can take one kind of music and make it your own by adding, subtracting or flipping it entirely around. What you do with your art is up to you." Does anyone know if a minister is available? She sends me out to get my own stuff and I come back quickly.

"I was thinking of mine while you got yours." I spread them out like they're playing cards. "Pick one, any one!" She closes her eyes and pulls out the first. It is a single by an artist named Marcaux called "The Over Under."

"This one I don't know."

"He's an up and coming rapper. The whole song is about how he deals with his mental illness. Did you ever hear a lyric that knocks you on your ass? Well, in one verse he says 'I don't like to express who I am outside of music, I've got depression that's seeping into my spinal fluid, plus I lost the only woman who would guide me through it, and I been praying that she ain't doing what I've been doing.' Though I don't have depression, I have anxiety that sometimes can make me make the dumbest choices and steer me off in a direction I would never drive in. I never considered suicide, but man this song hit hard with letting me know there's someone else out there." She looks at me with that look of "I've been there too." God this woman's awesome.

Next, we have Fleetwood Mac's album "Fleetwood Mac."

"Though God knows how many timeless songs are on this, it goes to show you can establish a following and support system in one iteration, then start all over again with new people and sound and come back even bigger and better. Not just in music, but life, too." She nods accordingly and says "Do you try and scare your first dates like this all the time?"

"No just the ones I really like."

She giggles and pulls out the last one. "Then lastly, Linkin Park's 'Meteora.'"

"Their first album everyone puts on their list of 100 albums to listen to before you die, but I so prefer this because they evolved so much in a short amount of time. Just goes to show if you do something once, you can do it again. And I prefer a lot of the songs on this like 'Breaking the Habit,' 'Faint' and 'Don't Stay.' Don't even get me started on 'Numb.'"

We go buy our selections then split to go to the comic book store. I realize she's consistent because she goes in and buys a hard copy of the collected works from The Amory Wars, the graphic novel series to the music of Coheed and Cambria written by Claudio Sanchez.

Then, we split towards dinner. I treat her like a gentleman and I hear this:

"Stop being nice. It makes me uncomfortable."

I make a stink face. "Why would it make you uncomfortable?"

"It makes me feel like you're expecting something at the end of the night."

"Angela, you know I'm not—"

"I know, I know but it makes me feel that way."

"So I'm damned if I do, damned if I don't."

"Now you're getting why I'm a single pringle."

"What if I am a gentleman, but drown it in sarcasm?"

She has a face of contemplation. "That could work." "So if I pull your chair out, for now on I'll say shit like "I know it's hard for you to do simple things on your own, hon," then peck you on the forehead?"

She laughs into her entrée "I love that."

I look at her fingers and notice she seems around a size 8. You don't let the one getaway guys. We finish our meals; I pay but let her leave a tip because I figured she'd kill me if I don't let her. I walk her to her car, give her a hug. For some reason, we don't let go. So I ask her, "Is someone expecting something at the end of the night?"

"Shut up. This is different."

I back up and say "I don't usually do that on a first date."

"Well, this is my first first date so let me make a mistake if I want to."

We have this kiss that makes planets melt. I don't know where she's been and I don't really care. I'm done with this dating and music life. It's all over and it'll never see my face again. Hey, that sounds like a hell of a lyric.

FIVE

Recording a Song You'll Probably Never Hear

I wake up the next morning elated. I have just had the best first date of my life. Is this how Ross and Rachel felt kissing in the rain? It must be. Speaking of which I need a shower. In all honesty, I keep thinking about her in everything I do. I even think about her as Bruce knocks his head on the door to drink some of the shower water.

Usually, at this point I'm highly overthinking what I do and the things I say. Having this much anxiety over such simple tasks is really irritating. Sometimes it makes me dizzy and frustrated. When it gets that bad my old mental health counselor used to say, "Just find a place to stand or sit, close your eyes and realize that it'll pass. A viable solution will come, you just can't see it right now." Wait a second, that's not a bad lyric.

Just so you all know, I am one of those freaks who can't help but write something down when it comes to him. I open my notes section of my iPhone and jot down for quite possibly the hundredth time a new set of lyrics. "One step forward, ten steps back, overthinking the things I lack," yeah that's not bad.

It's All Over-

Have I Been Here for way too long

pondering how I missed it all

turning the lights off they flicker they fade,

pondering all the mistakes that I've made,

and did I push myself too far?

Is it over?

Am I done Here?

Have I lived through, this hole that I've dug, waiting for you

I'm done here It's all over

You'll Never see my face

You'll never see who I am

Or what I have become

One step forward, and ten steps back

overthinking the things I lack

I constantly feel like I'm under attack

The whole world is spinning it all fades to black

And now I'm left alone, without you here to pull me out

Is it over?

Am I done Here?

Have I lived through, this hole that I've dug, waiting for you

I'm done here It's all over

You'll Never see my face

You'll never see who I am

Or what I have become

Why don't you just come over, you've always seen through me,
I'm not who you want me to be and you don't believe in me

I'm done here It's all over

You'll Never see my face

You'll never see who I am

Or what I have become

Why don't you just come over, you've always seen through me,
I'm not who you want me to be and you don't believe in me

Nothing helps inspiration more than a standard poodle moaning at you to take him for a walk or pay attention to him. "G'day, Bruce. We'll walk in a bit."

"I constantly feel like I'm under attack; while the whole world is spinning, it all fades to black." Being real with lyrics has almost become a form of journal writing. It gets the bad out to make room for more good. "And now I'm left alone, without you here to pull me out." Man, this song is hitting me like a flood.

I get out of the shower and call Tim to set up some studio time. Though we get along great, and in all honesty, he's probably my best friend, when he gets a call from me he knows that his work will probably go unnoticed since I've released absolutely nothing. Yes, I pay him his fee, but some take pride in their work. I'm getting there, but to some, they like to have something to show for their years of hard work. That's why I think when this is done I may try and at least get it copyrighted and maybe put it on YouTube at best. Give him something for his endeavor.

I get dressed and wait while chatting with Tim about what we'll need. I sit in Dad's chair; this big chair he uses for reading. The man inhales one good book per week so he needs his space for that. It's so comfortable, and he's kind enough to let anyone sit in it, but if he's got a book and a glass of milk, he'll just stare at you like, "You know the drill—up." Not even Bruce is sacred on that chair. He damn near comes with one of those brushes that umpires use to clean home plate: "Up, you stinking dog." I'm sitting and texting back and forth with Tim but I don't need to put his lamp on since I have the phone so it is a bit dark in the room. And here it comes again. Another bout of anxiety almost on cue. I suddenly have this feeling that I've been at this way too long and I've been missing the outside world and not progressing myself as a person. What am I saying? I know I have and that's the whole point of going back to school, but my anxiety is so strong that it makes me say this stupid shit that I know I don't mean. So, time to settle in.

I buckle down, put my head back to the edge of the chair and mutter to myself, "It will pass, it'll end, just hunker down until it ceases." Sure enough, it does. Obviously, it's my method, but whatever's legal and works for you, give it a shot.

I get out my notes and start jotting down the second verse. "Have I been here way too long, pondering how I missed it all? Turning the lights off, they flicker, they fade, pondering all the mistakes I've made, and did I push myself too far?"

This is how songwriting is, everyone. When inspiration hits, it hits. It takes time, elbow grease, and trial with a whole lot of error. It's not how everyone does it, but for me, this is it.

At around noon Tim opens up shop and gets everything warmed up. I pull up to the studio and in the meantime help him with his chores. By the way, the studio is in the basement of his parents' house. A lot of the glamour and show you see in Hollywood aren't exactly how most studios are. When you're starting out, often enough it's on a computer program in your bedroom or basement. I've even seen one in a greenhouse. There is nothing quite like getting drum sounds next to a bag of fertilizer. Talk about sounding like shit.

We bring everything down usually one or two items at a time. Today I brought the acoustic, one electric, an arrangement of five or so pedals, a bag of cords, and the amplifier, and that's a light load. From time to time I bring the keyboard, bass, or pedal steel, all with their own individual amplifiers. Luckily the basic recording I sent to Tim of the riff made him confident enough for him to use his own bass.

What most do is start with a drum track. They get the rhythm for the song and structure it before everyone else adds on their respective instruments or sound effect. Often, in my songs it starts with the guitar or vocals. Maybe from time to time a bass starts out, and since Tim's usually my drummer and is hearing the song for the first time, I'll start with whatever, then when he feels confident enough, he goes in and lays it down while I play into an amplifier that only he hears with headphones on.

What we do after all that depends on the individual song. This song is very bare-bones so we're using only the acoustic, the electric for one solo, and maybe the synthesizer on his computer for one or two notes on a keyboard with a certain sound effect that isn't available on mine.

Speaking of "bare bones," if you ever walk into a recording session and hear some of the musicians talk, you'd swear they were speaking another language of stupid similes and moronic metaphors—especially when using pedals and other things to alter the sound an instrument makes. Let's say I'm using fuzz, a sound effect used a lot in grunge or alternative music. I've heard people use it then say, "Man, that sounds like your guitar got dragged through mud then plugged in to make some music, right on." Can someone tell me why I'd do that? Hell, if I could do that I wouldn't have bought the stupid pedal. Or if I use some phaser and put a delay on, "Sounds like you're in outer space bro, righteous." If space had sound, people could probably hear you scream, so shut up and don't screw with good movie quotes. Let's say I was doing a heavy song that involved me using my voice to be more heavy-oriented, I swear to God you'd probably hear, "Your voice sounds like you're boiling screws and nails with lava from a volcano, dude." Need I say more? They mean well, but, holy shit, is it goofy.

We set up, hit "record" and each part is recorded individually. And I have to tell you, it came out great. Even he was impressed. This is the guy who has heard every song I've ever been willing to record. So of the songs I'm proud of, this is by far the proudest I've ever been.

To show someone a song you wrote, or any art for that matter, really takes a certain type of confidence. Art is the extension of your reality, so when someone hears a song you wrote and says, "Eh, I don't like it," it really kind of kills you. Obviously, there will be songs and other forms of art that don't speak to you and you yourself may even say, "This sucks." I've done it myself, even on the way over here. But just understand—if the time ever comes when someone shows you what they're working on, criticism is important, but be constructive. Tim may say that something sucks, but he says it in a way that's more palatable. He says "It's not for me," or "That doesn't speak to me the way you want it to." Even today, between the two verses of lyrics, he liked them but flipped the verses. He put the second verse first. Producing is one hell of a job that I want nothing to do with. God bless him.

I'm packing my stuff up when he comes in after being on the phone for quite some time. He looks me dead in the face and asks "how would you like to keep this going?"

"Dude, I'd love to, but I have a big day ahead of me."

"That's not what I mean," he says in a serious and optimistic voice. "You seem really on your game today, and if you can keep that up, I'll be happy to record and play on this for free. You don't have to pay me and we'll have an agreement to make it official.

I was flabbergasted. "Tim, you know I'd never let you do that for me. It's not right to do all this work for no money and I respect you too much for that crap."

"Doug, I think this is the best song you have and, in truth, you seem a lot different, in a good way. You seem more relaxed and with a greater perspective of who you are. I think the idea of never doing this again is making you take more chances and make better songs. I want to see where this goes. What do you say?"

You have to understand what all that means to me right now. This is his job, his trade and his profession. It's a very rare occasion when someone who does his job as well as he does offers to do it for free for the sheer reason of "I want to see it happen." It only happens so often. Good will like this is miraculously rare, and to not do your absolute best by that person would be a moral sinkhole. So though I promised myself not to get sucked back up into this business, not to subject myself to the inevitable let down of doing something creative for money, not to give my all to something that won't show me love back, I said "let's do it man."

SIX

Date Number Two: The Meaning of Ang

I know what you're all saying. "You just told yourself you'd never do it, you promised yourself, What the hell is wrong with you?" But that's the story of an artist. They think they have run out of ideas, but just like that, they get a good one and it's off to the races.

There's always the story of actors who talk about "Oh I did this play in high school, got the acting bug and I've been here ever since." And it's entirely true. The acting bug is basically the artist bug, it catches you and causes you to give everything you have, and to be left with nothing just for a few compliments. It's so strange and powerful. It's like chasing this high of "I can make it. I can see it and this time it will work." It's the power of an idea, good or bad. The only problem is, you can't see exactly how it's a good or bad idea until you bring it to fruition. You spend all this time and money to show someone your sense of self-expression, only to be left with this voice at the back of your mind saying, "Was it worth it?"

Sometimes it is, sometimes it's not. At one point I was in

three different bands. Each had their own different idea of their self-expression. One was a straight-up rock band that performed all its own original music. My idea was that this is the one that's going to make it and be a "success." I'll play the Garden with this band and tour the world. I can see it, absolutely. But here's the problem, I had the dream that an uncountable number of people have. I was thinking that mine was more important than theirs. Everyone has their own voice, that doesn't mean yours will sell well. It all fell apart after we all got tired of each other and gave up. We'd start bickering about who was in charge, where the next show should be played, how much money is paid to each member, and after a while, it stopped being fun. We were playing together purely because we got each other's vibe. Some people can work with each other without liking each other, but I just can't do that.

The second band was exclusively a "cover" band. We'd play anything the crowd asked for or whatever the vibe of the venue was. Whether it was a pool party, dive bar, or sidewalk: they asked for it, we delivered. It was all for money and that's it. It was fun, but we didn't see it as much more than a job that pays for the drinks.

The last one was bizarre. It was this concept band that was like a bad Coheed and Cambria or IF2112. The singer had written this sci-fi short story that he thought was excellent and wouldn't let us read until all the songs were done. When we read it, it was full of the same sci-fi crap that everyone uses. It had no originality and was really awful. We should have realized he had written the whole thing chain-smoking joints while listening to new wave music. He made us incorporate all of these instruments that none of us knew how to play and be experimental. Don't get me wrong, some of these bands are cool as hell like Coheed, Rush, and even Frank Zappa, but there's nothing more cringe-worthy than a really bad experimental band.

For every good idea, there seem to be about a million bad or half-assed projects. I can think of five of my own offhand that are too awful to comprehend or share. But just know that if your idea didn't cut the mustard, you aren't alone. Hell, I had a bad idea about the music driving to Angela's house to pick her up. I thought it would be a good idea to play a show with all my old songs just to show off the new one. Show seven bad songs to get to one good one? I don't think so, bud.

But I shake it off, park it, and text her saying I'm outside. She comes out and I get her door.

"Nobody ever gets me the door, thanks!" There she goes again, a compliment that makes me feel like shit.

"So what's the plan?" I ask.

She says, "Well, I thought about what your Dad told you: do what you love the most, and I couldn't help but love that. So my favorite thing to do when I'm alone is to get coffee and go for a walk. How's that?"

"Sounds great to me! Where is your favorite place to grab some?"

She opens up her maps app and types it in. We're maybe down the block when I get so eager about the song I have to just tell her about it. "So I don't know if I told you, but in my spare time, I'm actually a singer/songwriter. Mind if I show you something I'm working on for research?

To my surprise, she grits through her teeth and says. "Yeah, sure." I am a little taken aback, but I open the app Tim uses to send me things and start playing it for her. After a minute or so, her facial expression changes and she says, "This is great! Not at all what I was expecting." I can't help but ask, "Did you think I would suck?" She says, "I thought you were going to show me this rap you did on an app on your phone that sounded like crap. Like the really bad SoundCloud rappers."

And to be clear, this book is not anti SoundCloud rappers, but on the contrary, I like a lot of them. Some are talented beyond recognition, but oh my God, they make a bad name for themselves sometimes.

We arrive at the coffee place still laughing about it. We walk in and there's a bit of a line. We both chuckled at the little tip jar that says "It's bean a pleasure." Get it? Coffee beans? I'll shut up.

We pull up and park the car at this trail she told me she loves, and we go for a walk. While walking down the path we both point out similar things like signs, certain trees that are shaped weird, homeless tents, really showing how warped our senses of humor are. We even started holding hands while also making inappropriate hand gestures. We were two fucked up people falling madly for each other. We walked further along and stopped at this little lake to sit on a nearby bench.

"So I'm always talking about me, how about you tell me a little bit about you?" I ask, tucking my legs up on top of my knee as though I'm playing unplugged in a coffee house. All I need is a scarf, a beanie, reading glasses I say are prescription, and to hold my coffee with two hands and I'll be a hipster in Brooklyn.

She says plainly "There's not much to know about me, honestly. I'm into the arts as much as you are and I'm a nursing major."

"Woah slow down, Ang, you're too chatty," I say drooling with sarcasm.

She bumps my knee. "I'm not interested in talking about myself. If I had to tell you something I haven't told you yet, then maybe I'd like to travel more."

"Anywhere special?"

"All over the country, to be honest. I've never really left the state besides on a plane to visit my grandparents in Florida. My parents aren't big on leaving work."

"Well let me ask you, if you could travel to anywhere in the world, where would it be?" She puts her coffee to her lips and thinks it over. "I never really thought about where outside the country I'd go," she replies with coffee dripping down her chin. "To me, going out of the country was about the same as going to Mars, it's just not going to happen, you know?"

I am honestly really confused when she said this.

"To be honest, I'm okay with just leaving the state for a weekend just to check some stuff out. I get overwhelmed when it comes to new things, so only little bits of things at a time is all I can handle."

Now it kind of makes more sense.

"I've always wanted to perform in another country," I said taking a swig of my coffee. She perks up, "You totally should! Any chance you get to perform anywhere you should play. I read this one interview where this rock star said 'If you play anywhere and there's only one guy in there, you play your ass off for that sucker.'" I don't know if it's what she said or how she said it but I have to say, I'm pretty turned on.

Well, that's a good bit of advice; my producer talks about stuff like that all the time. "If they say play "Three Blind Mice", you play "Three Blind Mice" got it?" I say in a voice that sounds nothing like the guy, but it gets a laugh. Anything for a laugh, right?

"Does your producer always get on your case with stuff?"

"Not really, he's really cool and recently told me he actually believes in me for the first time. He wants to put more songs together and make something of them."

"That's awesome," she says in a higher pitch of excitement.

"Yeah it sounds fun, but I don't want to get my hopes up for the hundredth time. If we do anything, I want to do things differently. I know I say I want to perform in another country and all, but I haven't even tried to play out of state. We'd have to expand our market, not just play for the same five clubs in the area everyone knows me in. Maybe a music video or something we haven't done yet." She perks up and raises her hand saying "I volunteer to be merch girl."

I can't help but giggle. "You got it, babe" and I give her a big kiss. There will be plenty of times when I'll say, "Nothing is better than..." and say something. This will be no exception. There's nothing better than having someone be supportive of your ambitions. What's even cooler is someone who wants to volunteer their time to help you succeed and push you to be the greatest version of all you can be. Between her, Tim, and my parents, I have to say I'm one lucky son-of-a-bitch. There's always the part of me that will say 'Fuck you I'll show you!" to haters, but it has to be balanced with, "Thank you for being there for me." Gratitude has to be shown on stage at all times. Even in punk. Being too cool for the room gets old and people only seem to notice after the audience has already left. Always be humble towards those who put their money aside to be sure they can purchase a piece of your self-expression. You have truly nothing without them.

SEVEN

"No Pressure"

T hings could not be going better with Ang. We had the same things in common, the same pet peeves, and we started adopting each other's phrases and mannerisms. After a couple more dates like that, we decided to be exclusive. I was right about our instant connection and now I have proof. I even liked who I was becoming around her. I was more cheerful at work and wasn't an insufferable dick at home. The honeymoon phase was going great and I couldn't have been happier. But the honeymoon was about to come to a plane crash of a halt.

So was finally the end of the fall semester and the Christmas vacation at work. The principal of the school decided to have a Christmas party for all staff members and one guest each. Since Bruce was unavailable, I decided to take Ang. They were throwing it at a hotel instead of the gym since the last thing anyone wants to do is be caught sober. Obviously, you don't need drugs or alcohol to have fun, but we all love to talk shit about students and how we all hate our jobs, though it's the only thing we would do for forty years and tolerate it.

Black tie was optional, but fun was mandatory. Jesus, even Bruce could write a better slogan than that. Ang doesn't drink so she volunteered to pick me up. Modern women are the best, aren't they? Although it's best if they give you an inch, not to take the whole football field. She pulled up in this stunning black dress and a smile; I walked out putting on my jacket with an undone tie, and a flask in my mouth with my head tilted back to take a swig. I'm such a charmer it's sickening.

Her smile quickly turned to a frown. It turned to outright disgust when I give her a peck on the cheek, reeking of bourbon.

"Are you seriously showing up at this party like this? In front of your future colleagues and your bosses? You smell like a bar." I took out my cigarette since I only smoke when I drink.

"No worries. I'll change it to a smokehouse." I got in the car and she slammed her door shut.

"We're getting you some coffee to sober up before you get there," she said like I had no say in the matter.

"Sounds good. How was your day?"

"I'm not talking to you until we get there. Jesus, I haven't been this angry at someone in a long time, Doug."

I exhale my cigarette and say with sarcasm. "At least I know you care," but it was lost entirely. She slammed on the brakes and said,

"Take it back or I'm turning around." Now shit was getting serious. "I was being sarcastic, babe, I know you care, otherwise you wouldn't be mad. I'm sorry I overdid it with the pregaming." She noticeably lightened up but squeezed in one more line.

"Grow up, Doug."

Best "I forgive you" ever.

We grabbed coffee and along the way I cracked a few jokes to get her giggling. Now I was not totally sober, but I was getting away with it. We parked the car, she gave me a stick of gum for my breath, and we started to walk in. As we walked in, my coworker Brenda spotted me and said "DOUG." We whipped around to see this woman with a champagne bottle in each hand, mascara running, and a dress hanging so low I could count stretch marks near her areola. "Are you ready to get fucked up?"

I couldn't help but laugh and say, "Yeah, we're just trying to figure out how to pull your dress up, bud." She looked down, dropped the bottles and shattered them to pick up her dress. She looked down and started to cry.

"They were so young!" and she walked off crying. I turned to Ang and inform her that Brenda is the health teacher who specializes in drugs and alcohol. This is as much irony as one can muster for a lifetime.

We walked in and it was packed to the wall with people. So I started hammering them down to match Brenda, not thinking about the woman I was with or the conversation we just had in the car. I wanted to have fun with my friends, all the while disregarding the woman I loved the most. Boyfriend material, I am not. I turned around and notice she wasn't there. She wasn't even on the premises. She drove home and left my dumbass there. At least this girl had a head on her shoulders.

Initiating sequence, turbines to speed, loading program, and here we are! Loser mode! The state of mind I reside in the most. I just shunned the girl who could have been the one all the way home. Let's see the fabulous prizes. Why, it's a bottle of lotion, my left hand, and the Internet, what else could I fuck up today? Oh but wait, there's more! I just threw up the appetizers all over my father's suit. That's right, I can't even afford my own suit. I love my shit life deci—the rest of that sentence had been cut off by the second coming of vomit.

It's no secret that rock stars and their wannabe counterparts enjoy drinking the island of Ireland down to the last few drops. They get so demolished on a frequent basis to deal with their absolute shit self-esteem. Obviously, there are those who have a head on their shoulders, but that's all two of them. Most people who go into entertainment have the self-image of a banana slug. We have already talked about how they perform and make a group of strangers like them, but when they get off stage, they all go home and they're left with nobody but themselves. The loneliness gets overbearing and they drink to "feel happy." The truth is, booze doesn't make you happy, it makes you feel nothing. To some, nothing is better than pain. But contentment and self-love are better than anything else. If this wasn't a wakeup call as to how I could lose her, I didn't know what was.

I went up to my reserved room and fell asleep while the rest of the party enjoyed dessert. I woke up the next morning and

I'm so hungover that I could hear the carpet scrunching. I had never had a hangover as bad as this and I hope to God I would never get this way again. The only thing I could do now was assemble the clean clothes and put the dirty clothes in a laundry bag. So I put on my jacket with no shirt, pants with no underwear, and socks with no shoes. Looking like a big star right about now, huh?

I caught an Uber home and let myself in. Not even Bruce wanted to say "hi" because I smelled so putrid. I threw my clothes in the wash and hopped in the shower. No inspirational song now, just running water of the shower sounding like the blessed rain down in Africa.

I got out, grabbed three to four bottles of water and lay in bed, lifting my body only to drink whatever I could keep down. And I stayed there the whole day. I didn't get a text from Ang the whole day. That made the hangover feel like a halo by comparison. I called her about once an hour until eight in the morning the next day. I'm an overnight caller, that's how pathetic I am.

I felt well enough to get out of bed and drive, so I drove to get a greasy burger and damn near swallowed it whole. I just want to have something in my stomach to soak up the alcohol. I then zoomed over to Ang's to try and talk to her. I knocked and rang the doorbell for just shy of fifty-six minutes judging by how far the guitar neck had swung around my watch compared to the whammy-bar. Cool watch right? She finally came to the door.

She opened up and I started in on my bullshit. "Look I know what I did was fucked up and I shouldn't have been as bad as I was. You told me to cut it out and I ignored you and I shouldn't have—" and she looked past me the whole time. She did the coldest thing I ever saw. She picked her phone up and went, "Sorry, Mom, nobody's here. Nobody living to me, anyway."

Obviously, she was furious but there was a small part of me that thought "This is the end of it. The final nail in my coffin." I drove home. I had a stare that I never had before. The "my life is over" stare. Everyone has had it at some point in their lives. But this was the lowest I had ever felt in my life. My ended engagement seemed like Mount Olympus by the view from the bottom.

I got home and did the only thing that made sense. I went downstairs and tried to find the hit song I would never release. I don't know why, but this seemed like a good time to play acoustic. Maybe find the "I'm sorry" song I've re-written about a hundred times before.

I mentioned back at the studio about pedals that artists use to modify the sound or tone they play in, but let's take a tour of mine. In order of the proper layout, it goes filters, distortion, modulators, and time-based. I don't really play with any filters, but distortion and fuzz take up three pedals on my board of six. It can fit up to about twenty, but I'm not so high maintenance. Then I have one echo pedal, one reverb, and oddly enough, a loop pedal. A loop pedal is the master tool behind acts like Ed Sheeran, KT Tunstall, and Grace McLean. You step on it, play something, and step on it again in time when you want the loop closed. It will then play the loop over and over again. For some reason, I just felt drawn to it that day. I played around and found these two notes that I liked. I played them in a certain rhythm and then found some notes to harmonize with them. "Holy fuck, that sounds full," I said out loud to no one. I figure out the key and chord structure, and the words fell out of my mouth. "Roll me over, I'm not sober, I think I've had one too much. I've lost my brain, my life is in vain, and I've lost all self-control."

No Pressure:

Roll me over, I'm not sober

I think I've had one too much

I've lost my brain, my life is in vein

And I've lost all self control

You know I'm sorry for what I've said before

If you're not ready for me I'm out the back door

There is no pressure here, I want you to know

But these are the stories that I've been told

Wake me up, I'm fast asleep

You're my nightmare, you're nobodies dream

Tighten my grip, clench my teeth

You'll never see, what lis underneath

You know I'm sorry for what I've said before

If you're not ready for me I'm out the back door

There is no pressure here, I want you to know

But these are the stories that I've been told

You know I'm sorry for what I've said before

If you're not ready for me I'm out the back door

There is no pressure here, I want you to know

But these are the stories that I've been told

And if you could see me, for more than just a minute

You will finally realize why I'm never finished

There is no pressure here, just want you to know

These are the stories that I have been told

To me, if a song comes together so easily and almost on its own, you didn't write the song, it wrote itself, and came out through you.

I recorded it on my phone and send it to Tim. I received this text back, "Tomorrow at noon and we'll hammer it out. Don't show anyone else and we'll get the girl back with it." And we did just that. I ran over and we figured out I wanted to let Ang know there was no pressure to get back together with me. I know I fucked up royally and don't expect any forgiveness. Hell, I had coworkers text me stories of what happened. I got so wrecked. So once we figured out the last line in the chorus "there is no pressure here, just want you to know, these are the stories that I've been told," we named it "No Pressure" and Ang took me back on the condition that I seek help. So, I was on the gravy train of taking each day one at a time. It was already rolling, might as well blow the whistle.

EIGHT

Meeting Ang's Parents

I never had a huge drinking problem, but whenever I have gone out drinking, I have gotten absolutely obliterated. Just completely hammered. I could go months without drinking. But when I drank, I couldn't do it in moderation. After Ang gave me her ultimatum, I started getting help. I started eating right, going to the gym, I even started running. And I'm not a runner. It hurts my man boobs too much. But after I got the ball rolling, I started getting crushed by it. I started calling myself on my own bullshit. No matter what I do, I'll always want to be creative. I'm just wired that way. There's nothing wrong with it, just have to realize when it's an appropriate time. I learned through my meetings that I create a world making myself seem grander than I am. I don't want to have to get to know the world around me that doesn't get me. I'd much rather make my own world up with content that I can grasp. But you can't be so locked up in your own crap all the time that you forget you have responsibilities. There are people who rely on you and may need your assistance without a guitar in your hands. Yeah, the guitar is cool, but tough shit. You have to go to work, help Mom and Dad, and walk your silly poodle. You'll always have music and art, but responsibility comes barreling through the doors on occasion and you may have to give it up for a night to do something for someone else. Cue the next stage of my relationship.

So, Ang and I now have been dating for around three months: it's not a long time, but it is a noticeable amount of time to not have met the others' parents. I'm too chicken shit and she isn't sure if she's ready. Though I'd usually be upset or feel some type of shame, I'm in no shape right now to put myself on display like that for anyone. I'm doing too well, having too much fun in a new relationship, doing well in class and work, and experiencing the greatest revelation of creativity I ever had. Why screw it up? I'll tell you why. Standing still in life gets you nowhere, obviously. You have to keep going and looking for what's coming next, good or bad. To me, life is more or less like standing in the middle of the Colosseum as a gladiator. Taking on whatever comes next that's going to tear your ass apart. It could be a person just trying to throw a net over you and kick your ass that you have to put some effort into beating, a target you could easily spear, or a lion that's going to fuck you up and you have to accept it. Whatever happens, happens. Get over it and keep moving. This is a very long analogy for "suck it up and meet your girlfriend's parents."

She breaks the news to me quite gently though, I am at work tapping a kid's desk to focus when the bell rings and they all go to lunch. I am sitting in the lounge texting when there's a phone call to go down to the office because something is waiting for me. My anxiety peaks, hoping to God it's not a lion. I head down and notice it's just my girlfriend. So it's an easy target, but one that's fine as hell. She has even brought me fast food, something I haven't had in weeks. The only thing better than this is if she was going to feed it to me like Caesar with someone to fan me. Should have known it was bait to a trap.

"Oh my God, what a nice surprise. What're you doing here, babe?"

She hands over the bag with a big kiss. "I can't visit my boyfriend after class at his big job?"

"Of course you can! Just have to find this big job you're talking about." She punches my arm at the joke and takes me to go outside. "Let's go sit, it's beautiful out." Ladies and gentlemen, it's February on Long Island, the most un-nice out time of the year. This time of year it's nothing but grey skies, freezing temperature, but more than enough ice and slush to make anyone say "This sucks." We sit on this bench dedicated to who-gives-a-fuck and I start eating in the cold. I unwrap my chicken sandwich as a small bit of secret sauce gets on my shirt. But I have lost ten pounds so it still looks good on my dad bod-less body.

"So what're we doing for Valentine's, I ask as I wipe my shirt with a spit-filled napkin.

She takes my hands and says "I want you to meet my parents." I nearly dropped the sandwich. Nearly, I'm not a fucking noobie. I am, however, shaking my head already without words. She starts patting my hands and saying "Douglas, stay with me here. Douglas, babe." I hate it when she full names me.

"Babe, I'm not sure if I can do this." She gives me the "grow up" face. I swear she's like that thing from Avatar: the Last Airbender that revolves faces for something-or-another. I don't know what to say. I'm upset, pissed off.

"Babe, it's been three months. They're excited to meet you and they're really nice. I promise."

"You said the same thing about your friends," I retort with fear. By the way, her friends were boring as sin and thought I was too sarcastic. Humorless little twerps.

"My parents are different. They're very inclusive and a joy to be around."

"I think I need to lie down."

I pretend to faint so she rips my dramatic ass back up and says, "Don't be such a bitch." Now I know she's serious.

"Babe, do you love me?" She added sincerely.

"You know I do," I say, almost spitting out a pickle at her.

"Then we're doing this. Friday at seven, bring wine for them, and you drink water. Got it?"

"Got it, babe." I might as well have said "Yes, dear," and hung my head low, I felt so defeated.

"Alright. I'm going home. I'm getting cold."

"Why the hell did we come out here for this talk?'

She whipped back with a death stare and said: "I knew you'd

throw a tantrum so I wanted no witnesses if I had to kill you." Smart woman, that Angela.

Why am I throwing such a fit, you may ask? Because I'm an immature jackass. Yes, you already have that answer. But no musician has ever had a good encounter with parents of a significant other. It's just a fact of life. You see it in every sitcom. The dad's daughter brings home a boyfriend who's a leather-jacket-wearing, Harley-Davidson-driving, hair-slicked-back pretty boy who plays in a band and smokes cigarettes. What they all fail to realize is that in this day and age, musicians who grew up with the Internet can barely accept criticism, let alone be badass enough to walk into their spouse's parents' house and say, "Yeah, she's with me now, bro." I couldn't even text that to someone.

But that's just it. Time to grow up and start taking this relationship seriously. It took me six months to meet the ex-fiancee's parents. Although she was humiliated by me, so there is that.

I talk it over with Mom and though she understands the hesitation in taking such a leap, she has no understanding as to why I have such low self-esteem about it. I get done with my whole monologue—I told you about the TV version of me—and I hear from her for the first time in my life, "Cut the bullshit, Doug." That'll wake you up, huh?

"Mom, what do you mean?" She starts to pet the silly creature that now wants attention. As she scratches Bruce I hear his little bell around his collar ring and also the sound of my mother telling me how much she believes in me.

"Doug, look at who you are compared to who you were a year

ago. You were fat, unemployed, pining over a failed relationship and still thinking you were God's gift to music. I always had your back, but you were acting like a fool with no direction. It was humiliating. But you got back on your feet, got a job, and now you're healthy and full of drive and ambition. I've never been more proud of you than these last few months. You go to that dinner and you show those people the amazing son I raised." All the while a panting dope lays on his back for a belly rub with his tongue out full of joy. Pretty badass of her to tell me all that. I didn't know I was such a burden on them, for lack of a better word. But she is right. I've been kicking ass and taking names all year and I have something to show for my work. It's not an idea in my head or a riff that won't leave the basement. It's the true showmanship of a hard-working man. I worked my fingers to the bone to show people I'm not a loser and I can do it. And, hell, if I can do it, you can, too.

Although I really wish I had Mom's pep talk recorded. I could put it on my phone and play it as I drive down her street in khakis and a button-down shirt. I got wine and flowers on the passenger seat with sweat dripping down my face and into my eyes causing them to burn. Is this what my fuck buddies felt like? Pay attention, Doug. I park the car in front of their house like I've done so many times when they weren't home. I still hope they don't know I've been in their house, or their daughter. Sweat is rolling down my arms and I'm gripping the wheel as though I'm about to have a coronary, looking at my GPS, wondering how far Tijuana is. But I look in the rearview mirror and realize she has come out to the car to help me with carrying things in. She opens the passenger door, see's the flowers and says, "These for me?" I nod and she doesn't even smile, but says, "It'll look better if they're for Mom." She really is on my team.

I get out and on the walk up I see their yellow Labrador I've bought so many bones for without their knowledge. Sitting with excitement next to a stand with no vase next to it since we knocked it over getting so crazy making out and walking at the same time. She told me she blamed it on the wind knocking it over as she was opening the door. Is she a keeper or what?

We walk up her steps, since her house is one of those houses that has a scissoring staircase with an apartment in the basement. I'm greeted by her dad who actually has a smile on his face. What the hell is this? I shake his hand and I'm not nervous at all. I hand him the wine and it turns out to be his favorite. What fucking planet have I crashed on? I pet my friend, Lucy the yellow Lab, as I cross the threshold. I hand her mother the flowers and she pecks me on the cheek after giving me a hug. Is this what having likable people in your life is like? Hell, I'll come here for breakfast, lunch and dinner, if so.

All my notions about coming here tonight were wrong. And I couldn't be happier about it. It made every bad experience with the exes go away because I think in my heart of hearts I have found my people. We all sit and eat for hours around their big kitchen table. When meeting a potential mate's parents, it's almost like a job interview.

"So tell us, Doug, tell us about you." Mom's pep talk got me psyched to have the confidence to answer truthfully.

Instead of stretching the truth with "I'm an up-and-coming

musician with an album in the works," I tell her plainly, "I'm a teaching assistant at one of the local elementary schools while I'm in school for early childhood education. I have two lovely parents and a poodle named Bruce. In my spare time, I like to play music and write when I have the time." Her mom seems really pleased.

"Oh, Angela writes her own songs too! It's like June and Johnny Ca—"

"Mom, stop!" Ang damn-near gets up and covered her mother's mouth.

I looked over saying, "You never told me that."

"They aren't as good as yours and I can't play any instruments. It's more poetry, thank you, mother." She's blushing red and I wanted to laugh but don't want to embarrass her.

"Why don't you show me one of—"

I am cut off again when she shouted, "Show them yours." I took my phone out and show them "It's All Over" and "No Pressure." Her parents actually ask for a physical copy for their car.

I then ask Ang "Can I see your poems now?"

The little cheater goes, "I never agreed to it, so you lose." Jesus, she ought to be my contract manager.

Dinner is over and I stick around to help with the dishes. We all joke around telling old family stories and embarrassing tales from when we were kids. I did it. I faced the dude with the net I thought I was facing and kicked his ass. Ang and her mom go to the next room to grab a few cleaning supplies to which her dad grabs my collar and said, almost Batman-like, "I like you, you seem like a good kid, but if you make my daughter unhappy, I'll be sure you don't live to write another song about it." They are walking down the hall and he pushes me back up, both of us acting normal when they walk back in. Apparently, this lion still had claws.

NINE

"Oh Brother"

So after we have washed dishes and my neck is less red since I got pulled by my collar like Bruce when he poops on the rug, Ang walks me out. I stand in the garage and use my automatic starter before I go out. My night has been great so I'm not freezing my ass off in the meantime. "I think your parents like me!" She walks over and gives me a hug and a peck on the cheek. "I think they like you more than me. At least you can write a song." I pull her off gently.

"Yeah what's up with that? Why didn't you tell me you write songs?"

"I like yours more, so I don't want you to judge my crappy ones."

"They aren't crappy!" I said earnestly. "You haven't even heard them!"

"Yeah but they're by you so I bet they're great. If not, I'll help you."

"I don't want your help."

"Why not?" I said almost accusingly.

"Because they're mine. You, of all people, should know what your own sense of self-expression means to the writer. If someone comes along and goes 'I know you better than you know you,' it's kind of a dick move. Let me do what I want with them and if I need your help, I'll ask you for it." My car starts warming up; I give her a big hug and kiss on the forehead and say, "Fine I won't help. Only on the condition of you help me when I ask you."

"You mean *if* you ask me."

I gave her a kiss on the lips and said, "No, when I ask you. You mean a lot to me and I value your take on things." She blushed like the first time we met. "Okay fine." And off I go.

As I drive home I realize there are very few times in my life when everything has gone according to plan. This went even better. Who knew that all you have to do is calm the fuck down and things will sort themselves out? I can't help but notice on the way home that I'm driving with one hand on the wheel and my seat reclined back. I'm driving a little slower and I have a positive disposition. This is new, and quite frankly, I like it. I think I found the new Doug. Now back to our regularly scheduled program.

I pull up to the house and notice a familiar car in the driveway. A brand new out-the-showroom something-something sport with all the bells and whistles. It clicks in my head and my head falls on the steering wheel when I realize the inevitable shit hitting the fan and my good day comes to a screeching halt. My brother is home.

Now, my brother isn't a bad guy. Far from it. He's actually my best friend next to Tim. He's comforting and warm, with a kind sense of humor. Not a mean one like mine. It's just that he's successful and I'm—well me. He's the head of emergency medicine at the hospital Dad works at. Yeah, he got Dad the job. He stops over every once in a while to check on things when he has the time. Not that he doesn't want to, but he's booked solid while living at least an hour away. He's got a wife and kids, so it's not like he can just bail and come see us whenever. But every time I see his something-something parked in the driveway, I just know I'm going to inevitably feel like shit. He doesn't mean anything by it, it's my problem, not his. In fact, he's my biggest supporter. No matter how busy he is, he always makes time for my shows, listens to whatever I send him and gives me feedback that's constructive. It was actually his idea in "It's All Over" to switch the verses. Tim just backed him up.

I walk in at my normal height of six-foot-two inches, I will inevitably go to bed at a height just under the sidewalk—he makes me feel that small. Instantly as I walk through the door he's on me with a big bear hug. "How's it going, bud!" God, I love him.

"I'm good, Chris. Just got back from meeting the girlfriend's parents."

"Did you remember the wine I showed you?" See? The fucker is good.

"Yeah, it turned out to be her dad's favorite."

He claps his hands in approval "Told you, dude. It always works. Not too much burn just enough flavor. Just like

Robin." Robin is his wife. God damn, I wish I had his jokes. "Christopher!" Mom damn near throws a book at him. Yeah, he's an adult who saves lives every five minutes, but he's still her kid. Mom's house, Mom's rules.

"Hey how about we all sit outside with a fire?" Mom says with enthusiasm.

"Whatever you want to do Mom," Chris says. "Let me go get some old newspaper and we'll meet you both outside." Mom and dad get up and head outside all giddy. Not aware of the quiet storm about to brew between her sons. We watch them both leave. Chris takes a swig of the wine and says, "You have no idea how much I want your life, dude." Ding ding, that's the bell and round one starts.

I start with, "How dare you. You have everything I could ever want and everything I do, you do better in no time at all. Do you wish you had my life? Fuck you, man." He doesn't even get mad. Just shrugs his shoulders and says, "You don't think I'd rather mold the minds of America instead of saving the dumbasses that walk in every day?"

Oh, now I'm fuming. I go off with, "I basically point a kid's nose at his paper and say, 'Pay attention' for eight hours. Do you really think it's rewarding? You can do it walking in there with no experience. You save and improve lives every day." He starts to raise his voice a little.

"Drunks who decide I'm not worth their time or money, hypochondriacs who think they're dying of cancer because they farted a little louder than usual, and the chest pain who need a stent put in. Yes, it is a high-maintenance job but at least people appreciate what you do. Most people go on the

Internet and try and prove me wrong like I didn't go to school and put myself 250 thousand dollars in debt. At least you lived a little. Playing and writing music that everyone loves."

I kind of look at him funny. Not in a "Fuck you" way, but in a "Really?" kind of way. Like I never thought of it. Then he continues. "Not to mention you get to see Mom and Dad every day. You help them into their later years while I'm helping everyone else's parents. You get to see the fruits of your labor. If I do my job right, I don't see them again. But if I do see them, it's because they didn't listen."

I sit back; I never really realized he felt so unappreciated. It really hits me hard. This guy does nothing but gives while I take. And often, I do get more praise while he gets criticism. Like I'm supposed to whine about something that someone at a show once said about a song that took me ten minutes to rehearse? This poor fuck deserves more. I think I'm going to write a song about that.

I run outside and say, "Mom, I'm going to bed. Feeling kind of tired since that dinner." Chris heads over with his apology of "Look I'm sorry, I didn't mean to snap," but I am in full songwriter mode saying "Yeah, yeah. Sure, it's fine." I shut my door and pick up one of the acoustics. When I have a message and not a riff, I use the typical G-E minor-C-D chord progression just to hammer lyrics out. Over time I realize I want him to know it's okay and that he has responsibilities he can't help but have. He lives so far away and— "oh brother, how are you? I know that you're far away," yes a melody will outright interrupt a sentence.

Oh Brother

Oh Brother, how are you?

I know that you're far away

I know everything's so strange

Nothing is quite the same

Don't worry I get it, you don't have to say a thing

Life may not go your way, but you're stronger every day

But always remember

I'm just a phone call away

And remember

I'll always stay the same

Oh do you, remember

Our long drive through the north

You rested on my shoulder

We'll always be back and forth

Don't worry, you'll get it

Please don't change a thing,

I know sometimes you're angry

I love you all the same

But always remember

I'm just a phone call away

And remember

I'll always stay the same

We never wanted this way, but thats the way that it is

We can't be always thinking of wished for outcomes

We can't pretend that its easy, I think I got it from here

I'll all be worth it in the end

But always remember

I'm just a phone call away

And remember

I'll always stay the same

Moving on, I never really write songs about other people's struggles or their views. I always write my own views, even political songs. So I realize after I get this line, this is going to be a letter to him, for him, and about the struggles I now know he faces every day.

I send a rough demo to Tim. We developed a new system for recording. We only record on Thursdays so that Fridays are for Ang. But I am so nervous about how this will come out. What if Chris doesn't like it? What if it comes out like crap? But alas, just like before, my anxiety is subdued by the result of it coming out even better than "It's All Over." I show my parents and they cried, Ang and her parents think the same thing. So I send it to Chris. The thing is, I don't hear from him for a week. I nearly shit a brick. I call him after another studio session. "Hey, you never told me what you thought of the song," I say a little shyly. "Oh, God, it never sent!" he says in a panic. "I've been listening to it all week crying as you did after—" and I don't even hear him finish I am so elated. Jesus, what one song can do for another person. Not nearly as important as proper medical care, but it's really something. It just goes to show you never know someone else's life until you walk in their shoes. Hey, what a title, maybe that's something too!

TEN

Introducing Jackie III

So walking in my shoes turned out to be a bust. But it happens often. Nice of me to leave you with optimism then take it away, isn't it? Anyway, Tim and I have been working on a bunch of songs every Thursday after work. We have about eight or so finished but we're only going to do four—for an EP. In case you didn't know, EP stands for extended-play. It's a collection of songs more than a single with a B-side, but not enough songs to qualify as an LP or long play. A lot of artists do that these days to save money and to see how the first batch of songs performs. If they like it, more come. If not, well you get the idea. We know "It's All Over" and "No Pressure" for sure are going on it. I'd really like the song I wrote for Chris, "Oh Brother" to go on it, but it's up in the air. We have a lot of options to work through. Many bands make damn near up to fifty songs for an LP of about twelve songs. Artists like John Mayer, blink-182, and Green Day all come to mind. It's better to be over-prepared than to go forward and be told we don't have enough. A goal I always set out to accomplish is that every song you put on an EP should have the potential to be a single. No songs that you could skip over or say it's an "album song." And I have to say I'm pretty proud of what we have as a product. Even Tim is getting more enthusiastic than usual. So enthusiastic that he did something I damn near killed him over.

I got a call from him the other day saying "Hey, man, so I really like how this is going." I replied, "Hey, dude, me too." He went on to say "So I've been showing a lot of people it and I'm getting nothing but positive feedback."

"That's great!"

"Yeah, I sent it to a few people I used to work with." Now if you're not into the business aspect of songwriting I can understand why you wouldn't get why I was enraged. To send a song out that isn't copyrighted is extremely dangerous. Anything that isn't copyrighted runs the risk of being stolen and not having proper legal backing to say, "I own this, this is mine." So for Tim to be so careless, was to me, blatantly distrustful. And I let him know it, too.

"Are you fucking crazy? You know none of these are copyrighted and there are one of two people on your roster I've heard use one or two of my riffs, Tim. I cannot believe you'd do that." But he was all cool about it.

"Don't worry. None of them would fuck with my productions or steal from us. In fact, they asked if you'd have the time to sit down with 'Jackie Ill' and help her write the hook for her new song.

"I still think she has the dumbest name."

"She's offering to pay you."

"Tell her she's got a deal." I'm a sound whore, what can I say. The only hangup I have is, Jackie Ill is a 21-year-old girl whose becoming something of a local legend. She has featured on all these artists' songs and is really starting to blow up and has all this sex appeal. And as a 26-year-old man, I have no idea what it's like to be a pretty 21-year-old girl. So I go to the prettiest 21-year-old girl I know.

I call Angie up and ask her to send me a few of her lyrics. And boy, that wasn't an easy fight. "Ang, I really need to see a few examples. I have no idea what it's like to be this girl." Her response was "because I do?"

"Ang I have no idea how to sound like a 21-year-old girl with boy problems. I don't know if I can relate to her or write in her style." And thank God she's the brains between the two of us because she lays it out for me. "She doesn't need another song that sounds like her. If she's coming to you, she wants to sound like you. So just let her talk about her life for a little bit and make what you can make of it. If she likes it, she'll take it —and I'm sure she will. She wouldn't be paying you money if she wasn't." God, I love this woman. So Jackie comes to Tim's studio in a limo. Mind you, she lives four blocks away. Fucking divas.

She comes out of the car with a security guard and a Maltese in a crop top, mini skirt, and sunglasses. Keep in mind, it's raining. I have no idea what a lot of artists like this are thinking. But then again, maybe that's why I'm still here. But this is a recording session, not the VMAs. I go to sessions in the plainest and most comfortable clothing I can find. Hell, I'll go in sweatpants and a hoody if I can still sing. I'm not out to impress anyone with anything but talent. She doesn't walk in at first, she has the security guard circumnavigate the perimeter of the studio, all three rooms, making sure there isn't anyone conspicuous. Fucking ludicrous. Then she walks in soaked but acts like she meant for it to happen.

"Which one of you is Doug?" she says to the two of us, fully aware of who Tim is. "That'll be me, dear," I say through my teeth, full of frustration. "I like that one song you do with the guitar and I wanna have lyrics like dat." Keep in mind, she's putting a Latino accent on and this girl is whiter than Dove soap. I lost it after that. That's right, two sentences are all it took. "Okay listen, I know you want me to write a song for you but I am not going to put up with this horse shit image. I don't know you, but I can see right through this crap and know this is not who you are. Maybe your self-esteem is shit and you're trying a new image because you're terrified of showing your real one but you must be a real asshole to suppress the real you. No way are you getting one of my songs." She busts out crying and shows who she really is. Someone exactly like me.

"Fine. I'm sorry I wasted your time. I really liked your song and it sounded like something I've always wanted to do but never had what it takes. I'll leave; goodbye."

Tim looks at me as she runs out the door and goes, "What the fuck was that? Are you trying to be an extra-special asshole? Go get her outside or you and I are done."

So I haul ass after her. "Dear, please stop. I'm sorry. I didn't mean it." I'm shouting this as I chase her the four blocks back to her mother's house. She goes to her house and slams the door. I knock to be greeted by what I can only describe as a brick wall with limbs, an earring, and a really pissed-off expression that speaks with an Italian accent.

"What did you do to my Jacqueline?"

"Sir, I apologize. She was speaking weird and I lost my cool. I'm here to say 'I'm sorry' and hope that she'll come back and get some work done."

"She's not going anywhere with you now. Get off my property." I go for broke with this guy. "Sir, she was acting in a way that didn't sound like who she was at all. I don't know her, but I know when someone is doing something they don't want to do. If she doesn't want to come back, fine, but at least let me tell her I'm sorry." She calls from inside the house

"Daddy, it's okay. You can let him in." He gives me that same weird stare Ang's dad gave me at their house over dinner. I walk in and she's in their living room with tears running down her face.

"Hi, Jackie Ill. I'm sorry if I was a—" she interrupts and says, "Don't call me Jackie Ill. That's not my name."

"You don't like your own stage name?" She gets real as hell with me.

"My manager picked it out. I'm not even a hip-hop fan. The only way he'd manage me is if I changed everything about myself and went under this title and image. It's not what I want to do at all."

"Well, what do you want to do?" She has me sit on the couch.

"I want to be the next Stevie Nicks. I want to play music like

Fleetwood Mac, Tom Petty, and Bob Dylan. Stuff with a message that matters. To be there for other people like they were for me. But they told me maybe when this hip-hop faze wears out I can do what I want. But until then, it's all about going with the trend. That's why I loved 'It's All Over.' I told my manager you were the writer of that song about bouncing asses off the wall so maybe you can write a folk song that was so good he'd change his mind and let me do my own thing."

I take a big breath and exhale. "Jackie, let's go write your new song. I've already got a theme and a verse in mind." She gets excited and gives me a big hug. I couldn't have been more wrong about her as a person. We get back to Tim's and we get to work.

Turns out she has been at war with herself and her own image ever since she started trying to make it as a singer. Like many pop and hip-hop artists, her label and management want them to be what's trendy, to have sex appeal, and to make songs played in clubs that people drink shots to. After she says the words "at war," it came to me. I play this very Neil Young acoustic riff with a harmonica and sing, "Oh the last time I left for war, I learned a thing at my hell's front door. Those who do not know their own worth, are living in their own hell on earth." She starts tearing up and runs into the booth to sing it. We have to remind her we need to lay down all the instruments first. But it is so nice to see someone be herself after such a long time being someone else. She is damn near squealing she was so excited to have it her way. We go on to write the whole song, but my favorite part is "live your life, but not too fast, you never know how long you'll last. Be your one and only self, you're the only one, there's no one else."

Tim sends it off to her manager and it is almost like he ordered a salmon and got a steak. He is so irate he called Tim in a fervor. Tim tells them they already spent their money on it so they might as well put it out. Scenarios like this usually call for a lawsuit big enough to make a grown man cry, but everyone at the label loves it so much they don't have the heart. It technically is their property, so they make it a little faster, add sampled drum beats instead of Tom's outstanding playing, and take out the bridge of our harmonies and made her do a rap verse over it. It sounds more like "Over and Over" by Tim McGraw and Nelly. I hate this business.

ELEVEN

You Sure You Want to Be Famous?

Wow, I did something productive with music. That's a first. It didn't go to number one on the billboard charts or anything, but it's been getting some airplay on college radio stations. Better than anything I ever did on my own. I kept getting calls from Jackie saying, "We did it! It's on the radio. Thank you!" It was cute at first, but after the tenth time, it gets under your skin. But I can't really bitch. Since they didn't get rid of the audio of me harmonizing and the one or two vocal lines I threw in, it is dubbed "I'm at War" by Jackie Ill featuring Doug Manning. I am getting phone calls from relatives I hadn't talked to in years because it was played on a college radio station that broadcasted on the same channel as a national sports team. Isn't that nuts? From a guy who was slowly backing out of the business, I sure as hell seem elbow deep in it.

Speaking of which, Mom and Dad were not so thrilled. Seeing that I'm working and going to school full-time, it seems like I'm not taking everything seriously. Mom approaches me nicely about it. "Heard your song, Dougie. When did you have time to write that?"

I countered with, "Kind of just wrote it in an hour, Mom. She hit me with a wave of inspiration I was feeling at one point, too. So it just came naturally." That went as well as could be expected.

"Well have your grades been coming to you so easily?"

I rolled my eyes while her back is turned. "I just have to finish a paper on the progress I've made since starting my first semester. A real hand-job of a paper, Mom."

"Will you just take this seriously!"

"Mom, you're not in the class, it's easier than you think it is."

She almost drops the boiling pot on my head. Deservingly so, since I am being a little snot. "You know what, I'll just go out for a while. I'm taking everything seriously. I wrote a song for someone, that doesn't mean I'm quitting my job or dropping out of school. Please chill." Please note, you should never tell anyone angry to chill, because they will erupt with anger. Especially the woman who gives her entire life for your existence. Yeah, I've earned a piece of shit, gold medal.

I get in the car and start driving. I have not even traveled two blocks when I get a call from Dad. Oh boy, did I fuck up now. I answer with a pleasant, "Hello?" In return I get, "So this is what's going to happen. You're going to turn around and drive home to apologize to your mother for your shitty attitude. You know you haven't been giving work and school your full attention and it's about time you do. We have been beyond patient with you about music and I'm putting my foot down. You've gone too far." I went from pleasant to enraged within .05 seconds. "What the fuck did I do here? Yes, I'll apologize to Mom but I didn't sell drugs or wreck the car. My grades are great, work loves me, I'm doing better with my health than I ever thought I could. Get off my back. It's my life," and I hang up the phone.

And if you think Ang is on my side, oh you'd be dead wrong. More times than not, my girlfriends have always taken my parents' side. Win, lose, or draw, they'll never be on my side. It gets quite annoying, actually. I pull up to her house and she's waiting outside for me. Jesus are they all on a conference call? I'm not even out of the car when she's at the window with her hand out with a phone in it. "Call your mother, now."

"Babe how did you—"

"She called me," she says, interrupting. I don't know if I can get a word in edgewise in my own life. "Ang, I'll call her later I just want to blow off steam and get my head straight." "You don't get to cool off with me until you call both your parents and apologize." Now I've lost all my cool. "I don't want to hear it from any of you. Don't forget, you told me to write to her and gave me some pretty great advice on how to. This 'hit' is on nobody more than you, Ang. I'm sick of everyone talking to me like they're in charge of me. It's my life and I'm going to live it how I want to."

"Then drive off because I'm not talking to you for the rest of the day, asshole."

I didn't even say "bye". Just put the car in drive and drove off.

I'll talk to mom and dad later, and I'll apologize to Ang tomorrow or something. I don't want to go home, but I can only think of one place left to go. So I stop by Chris's place. I am greeted at the door by him but with a look of absolute disappointment. He shakes his head silently but saying everything. We say nothing to each other as I got back in my car and head down his driveway at full speed. I have nobody on my side. The support system that sent me hurtling toward this world is now pulling me back because it has become bigger than they thought it would ever go. It's almost like they are all saying, "He's having fun, why ruin it for him? It'll never happen, so what's the harm in him having fun?"

I'm not allowed to go home, but I have no place left to go. So I stay in a hotel for the night. I can't believe what I'm reduced to. What a cliche I've turned into - a lonely artist in his hotel room. I have some bouts of inspiration, but nothing concrete comes of them. I've never been kicked out of the house before, but here I am.

The next day I go off to work in the same clothes I wore the day before. Yes, I have washed them. I'm not a total pig. I get a call from the class I'm in to go down to the principal's office. I've never been to the principal's office, even as a kid. So obviously, I'm petrified. I walk the long walk of shame down the main hallway past the guidance counselors, the school nurse, and the auditorium. And maybe it is the sheer panic of this possibly being my last walk down this hallway that has scared the shit out of me enough to realize that I don't want to lose this job. It's a good gig while I'm in school and It'll only get better as I grow older. Why blow it on a gig that'll get sick of me and throw me to the scraps when they find the next-best replica? Jobs like this value wisdom and experience, they don't discard them. Everyone's right, I have to get my head out of my ass and into the sun where I can see what's coming next.

I walk into the office and have to re-introduce myself to the office assistant. Now I'm not against hiring the elderly to do clerical jobs, but I think to qualify for this job, you should have to be able to see the person coming in for assistance. Have your bifocals ready, Darleen, we have shit to do.

I walk in and Max, the principal, who I graduated with by the way—over-achieving prick—sits me down to have a talk. He's nice enough but feeling inadequate in everything you do in life sucks. Having someone speaking to you in a shallow and pedantic way doesn't help.

"Hey, Doug, have a seat." So I sit like Bruce waiting for a treat.

"How's Mom and Dad?"

"Everyone's good. Getting together with them later for dinner," I reply obviously lying.

"Girlfriend good?"

"Yes, sir. Just got back from a vacation."

Artists lie every day to make it look like they aren't scrounging.

"And how's Chris?" "Everyone is good, Max, what's—" he gives me a look with the intent of letting me change what I just called him.

"Sorry Dr. Veitman, slipped into old high school jargon."

He doesn't say anything, just nods his head. "So I was listening to the radio and I have to tell you about this song I heard. Seems like you finally broke through and I have to say I'm proud of you."

I'd be smiling and saying 'thank you' if I didn't expect it to be followed by some bad news. He could have said this in the hallway, why call me to the office? Then he turns around and sits in his chair. "It's really great. I love how it sounds, but I don't like the sound of my students talking about one of my TA's being a pop star on the radio. It's a distraction and gets rumors started."

I squint my eyes with disbelief. "What rumors are you talking about, dude?"

He rolls his eyes, seeing I'll never fully respect him. "How about that you wrote that song snorting coke off her ass, or you're leaving to go on tour with her? Or how you both are hosting SNL as a couple."

"Wait, you know none of that is true."

"Yes, Doug, I know. The point here is you can't keep doing both. The school board is pressuring me to fire you."

I damn near fell out of my chair. "Fire me? For what, having a hobby?"

"I told them the same thing, I can't fire you for something legal you're doing in your spare time. But, we can fire you for causing distractions to students and displaying inappropriate behavior."

"It's not even my behavior!"

"Rumors can overshadow the truth and you know that."

"So I'm just letting you know, it's going to have to be one of the other. Teaching, or music. I'm sorry. I wish I had another choice. Head back to class and try to have a better day."

I walk out, stark white and pale. It wasn't just a metaphor anymore, I have to make a choice: have financial security and be stable doing something I love, or do what I've always wanted since I first dropped the needle on a turntable.

I drive back home and pick up flowers for both Ang and Mom while I grab candy for Dad. I think I flipped between the right choice and the wrong choice at least a hundred times today. But then again I also think I made the right choice. I'll never know until I pursue my pick and see in the end. Jesus, I know people make hard choices like this every day, but this is never something I was prepared for. Regardless, time to man up and apologize to the people I love. The people who, no matter how angry they make me, are just looking out for me —regardless of how much they're being a pain in the ass. I roll up to the house and to Ang's car parked in the driveway. Are they hanging out without me? What the hell? I walk in with everything and they're on me in a second with hugs and kisses.

"What the hell is going on?"

Dad put his head on my shoulder. "Doug, Tim died early this morning."

TWELVE

"Long Long Gone"

You could have knocked me over with a feather. It was almost like a part of my soul was ripped straight out of me. My best friend, the 23-year-old genius producer, dead. You ever hear something that devastates you and it's so unfathomable it's like you didn't hear it? After Dad told me, it was like he had said it in Latin. I just made a face and acted like it wasn't what he said.

"Dad, w-what did you say?" He gave me a big hug, let go and said, "Tim was riding his motorcycle when a 90-year-old with dementia blew through a stop sign and hit him. He was pronounced dead at the hospital after they tried everything. It happened just up the road about a mile away." I fell to the ground. I just lay on the floor without any intention of getting up. The guy who truly believed in me as a human being cut down in his prime by someone who shouldn't have been on the road. What the hell is wrong with this world? The good really do die young and we leave the assholes to live forever.

I lay on the floor crying for about an hour and 17 minutes. It could have been 20, but my watch had tears on it so it was tough to read. I tried to call Tim's phone at least 10 times in that hour. I'd heard of people doing it, but I couldn't help hoping that he would pick up and it was just like a death hoax from the Internet. I even messaged him some old riffs to see if he'd respond. But no, he was long gone. I did get a message from Jackie, though. She was as distraught as I was. I got a bunch of messages from all the artists he worked with. All stuff about how he was an outstanding producer and just really good to artists. But honestly, Jackie and I were the only ones talking about Tim the human being. The guy that would call an Uber for you if you were short on money for a ride. The guy that boosted my self-esteem if I was ever feeling down on myself or my abilities. It really goes to show that you'll only be shown the respect you deserve when you're gone. Only when you can't hear are nice words said.

The funeral was a week away. Tim's mother was so distraught she was in denial up until two days before. She kept saying things like, "That can't be him. He's on vacation," or "He's at his father's house all week." Unfortunately, Tim never knew his dad and he had only ever taken one vacation in his life, three years ago. Even then he brought a guitar along with him just in case something sparked.

I pulled up to the funeral parlor with Ang. She hadn't let me out of her sight since I got off the floor. I was gripping her hand like a kid so I wasn't showing much progress. Walking in we realized were about 10 minutes early. If there were too many people I probably would have bailed because oddly enough, I don't do well with big crowds without being in charge of them. So maybe it was a blessing in disguise. We walked into the room where the funeral was to be held and only a few people were there: This one cousin I had met once before and his parents. I gave my respectful greeting, sat down and just waited. The doors opened so we stood arms folded. Turned out to be his mother being escorted in by two other family members. She looked like she was about to fall to the floor and had to be held up. I'd been there already so I was about to join. Then they wheeled in the coffin. I was so not ready for this. He was wheeled in by about 5 family members. One of them seemed to be about 14 or 15 and he seemed awfully scrawny and emotional so the casket was listing to the right while going down the aisle. So I walked over Ang's legs, walked up, and straightened it out while walking him down the rest of the way. Tim had guided me God knows how many times, time for me to return the favor.

We lined him up the way you do at open-casket funerals. They popped the top open and he laid there still. Even hanging out with the guy he always bounced his leg as he had restless legs. Seeing him this still almost made me not believe it was him. They put in the belongings that meant the most to him. A childhood blanket he stuffed his bass drum with, a picture of him and his mom from his first concert. And the AC/DC wristband he'd had since he was a kid, allegedly the only thing his father ever gave him. Lastly, they put in this china cymbal he made out of a kids toy from the church he played at. This friggin' bizarre-looking thing. Every time we jammed I'd make fun of it but he always had the same answer. "Yeah, it sounds like shit, but I made it, man." I stood over him with my head down and hands at my front and said, "Rest in peace, man. I love you," and I walked out. I couldn't handle this.

I had Ang drop me off home and told her just to go. I needed to be alone for the weekend. I went to my room and shut the door. I didn't come out for a good 10 hours. I came out just to eat dinner, then went back in. I didn't go to the basement once. Why write songs anymore? I can't captain a ship without my first mate.

I got out of bed finally around Sunday afternoon. I started to walk and I had to catch myself for fear of falling over. I caught myself on my dresser that had my stereo on it. I accidentally hit it on and all of a sudden the stereo jumped to this track of us screwing around into the microphone. Just yelling and cursing with funny accents with Autotune. Just being crazy kids, having fun in the studio. I couldn't help but giggle like a little girl. I knew I would always have these recordings and memories of us making music, but I wished I could have one more minute with him to just say thanks. Just to write one more song, one more memory, and tell him how much he meant to me. My brother from another mother. Since I don't have him, I'll write one for him.

Tim always got on my case about trying to branch out with new instruments. Even if it was a piano.

"Everyone's heard you play guitar, dig deep, bitch, branch out once and awhile." So I ran over to the piano with my guitar, playing these four chords he always liked. I looked on the neck where the notes were and figured out the tempo on the piano. I started playing the chords whole, but it sounded too busy, "Maybe it'd be good for the chorus? I don't know." But then I remembered he always liked it when one hand stayed the same while another played the bass notes. So I gave that a shot and I figured out the verse then and there. As much as I liked these chords, the song seemed really bland and kind of boring on its own. No matter what words I put over it, it was kind of bare. Any guitar part I write for it just sounds too busy, so maybe the drums will be constantly changing and that would almost be the interesting part. Like never having the same drum part in any verse or chorus. Regardless the best drummer I ever worked with had recently died, so I guessed it was up to the few drum lessons he had given me to get me through this quagmire.

After I had got up and made a cup of coffee I got a call from an unknown number. Same area code, maybe a town or two over, but I answered anyway. "Hello?" as you typically say. The voice on the other line was a woman who sounded familiar. "Hello. Is this Doug?"

"Yes it is, who may I ask is calling?"

"Hi, this is Ms. Fallon, Tim's mother."

"Oh, um, hello, ma'am. I'm so sorry for your loss and to be acquainted this way. How may I help you?"

"Well, I'm sorry to be a bother, but it seems you're one of the few numbers he had in his emergency contact book. Did you two record often?" Tim's basement was soundproof so anyone playing was never heard upstairs.

"Yes, ma'am I was over every Thursday for about the last three months. We'd go out together on the rare occasions we'd both have the energy to get up and we've been friends for many years."

"Oh, well it seems like I found the right person to call, then."

"What do you mean, ma'am?" I was seriously confused.

"I was wondering if you wouldn't mind taking his recording equipment out of here. It's become far too painful to look at and it'll do no good here by itself with me. So I figured if anyone should have it, it should go to someone he deemed important enough to write down for an emergency." This took the air out of my chest, I had barely any idea how to work any of that crap, but if this poor woman is suffering, I really ought to take it off her hands. "Yes, ma'am I'll be over within the hour." I called Jackie and we both went over to dismantle it all.

As we walked in we're greeted by her in pajamas, a robe, and no makeup on. She'd probably cry it all off anyway but you could tell she'd been in a world of pain by the redness under her eyes. They matched mine. So we walked down and she said, "Take everything out except the drum set. That I want to stay with me.

"Yes, ma'am," we both said at the same time. We went through everything, the crap wires he'd kept in an attempt to fix them, the headphones from the mid-nineties he thought were vintage, and God knows how many broken drum sticks he, at one point, had tried to hot glue together to make a chair. Spoiler alert, it broke instantly and had sat on the ground broken ever since. We picked it all up and took some of the posters of the bands he was in off the wall. Thought it would be nice for his mother to have them framed.

We chucked the broken sticks in a garbage bag, took the drums upstairs to vacuum the rug they were on and the rest of the basement after everything was done. We loaded the cars up with box after box. Then went back in and said goodbye to Tim together in the basement. We went upstairs and said goodbye to his mom. As I pulled away I couldn't help but look at his house in the rearview mirror. It was the final moment of realizing my friend was long, long gone. Oh, wait a second...what a title.

Jackie and I went back to my place, plugged in the bare essentials and hammered out the song very quickly. I still had Dad's drum kit so I figured out some ambient beats to fit the straightforward patterns. It was almost like drumming when necessary and in good taste. Jackie and I made it a duet. I almost couldn't make it through when she wrote: "now you'll always be 23 years old, now you'll always be out in the cold."

Long Long Gone

I know you've heard it from your mother before

Put it down once you close your car door

It can wait for a second it can wait for a minute

My life way way better when you were in it

Now you're long long gone

Now you'll always be 23 years old

Now you'll always be out in the cold

I just had hope I could make the wrong things right

Guess I'll try to stay awake through the night

Now you're long long gone

You can peel the rubber from the streets where you were

Just a mile up the road I hope you just weren't hurt

My friend for so long and now its come to an end

You were way too young you were way too young

Now you're long long gone

Jesus, even now it makes my bones ache. We had something that would immortalize our mutual friend: the friend that brought the two of us together as artists and souls with the same dream and ambitions. I'll always love my friend and miss him more than I can bear. I just wish I had one last moment to tell him one thing. I could write it down a million ways but I'll always come back to, "What the fuck is up with that cymbal, dude?" Some things will just never change.

THIRTEEN

God Dammit Champ

Jackie and I decided to produce the song ourselves with what little knowledge we had between us. Tim and I had written and recorded together for years so every once and a while I'd hear him mention things like, "Double tracking each instrument to make it sound fuller." Or "If you play with the Les Paul, do a second guitar track with the telecaster." And also "Apply the EQ to get some clarity." It all amounted to the last song I'll ever record. Oh, that's right, I didn't get to mention my decision about what to do with everything involving Tim. I am throwing in the towel after I releasing this one EP. I am going to make this a tribute to Tim and put it out under the alias "Panic Under Pressure" to be sure work doesn't find out.

I liked the way the song had come out, I have to say. I even showed it to Ang and she thought Tim had done it himself, so that was a good sign, right? Even though we all know I'm not continuing on after this, I want it to be right. God forbid I ever have kids, they can hear it so they know their dad doesn't totally suck. He is actually pretty tolerable. Ang and I ended up getting together to decide which of all the songs sounded the best. Even though there were some good contenders, "It's All Over," "No Pressure," "Oh Brother," the new one for Tim, "Long Long Gone," came out the strongest. I guess we burn brightest near the end and want to show we did our best when the inevitable end is coming. Whatever the case, if this was what I was left with at the end of the day knowing I could do no more, then I would be satisfied with what I have.

I'd written the best I could for myself, Tim, and Jackie. I'd been unhappy with life before and I guessed this was the highest note I can go out on. I wished I had my friend to see it end with me, but what can you do? That's life, unfortunately. Sometimes those who stick by us through the worst won't get to see the end result. It's an awful feeling, but it happens. Tim had told me he was proud of what we were making at the end. So in hindsight, how can any review hold up to that?

About a week after we got everything mastered by a few of Tim's old associates, I got a call from an unknown number. I answered and instantly thought I was either on a game show or that the other person was mentally ill. I picked up the phone and heard, "Hello, Doug. This is Champ Beats with Management Unlimited. How the Hell are you?" I damn near gave my own phone a stink face. "I'm fine, sir. How are you?"

"Well, I'm quite fantastic after hearing this EP of yours." Now I was mad. It wasn't supposed to be given to anyone outside of myself or Jackie.

"Excuse me. Those songs are not for release."

"No, I'm not releasing them, sir. I'm here to represent you."

This was really bizarre, although not unlike the luck that I usually have when it comes to life decisions. I would get out, and they would pull me in. "Mister, um, Beats? Is it? How did you hear these songs?"

"Well your friend Jackie was holding onto them and I listened to the mastered tracks on her computer. I'm her manager, you see."

"Sir, I haven't even heard the masters. I can't help but feel this is a complete violation of my privacy."

"Well, don't get so upset sport. You'll be rich and famous with these songs. I can guarantee that."

"I don't want to be rich and famous, these songs were made for my release and on my terms. The answer is no. Piss off."

Managers and people who do the representing in this industry are notorious for going too far, making promises they have no intentions of keeping, and ripping people off. I have zero trust in someone who has no respect after hearing "no," and continuing on anyway. Fucking pigs.

And just as expected, it wasn't the last I heard of him. I got a call two hours later from him to sign a 360 deal. I immediately shot him down. Two hours after that, I was asked to sing on another song with Jackie under my real name to keep with the hype of "I'm at War."

"Forget it. Go away. If it's not on my terms, I'm not doing shit. Goodbye." Four hours after that, he went for broke. "Alright, kid, what do you really want? Nobody makes music like this because they're bored. They must have something in it for them." Wow, now he had caught my ear. Besides the big "fuck you" I would inevitably give him before the call ended, I did have one request before I packed it all in. I wanted to do one show at the biggest theater in town, the Roundhouse. It's a 2000 seater that only national acts get to play. No locals allowed ever. I would have loved to play that with the songs on this record there, plus a few with Jackie, and a cover or two of mine and Tom's favorite songs. After that, I would be gone. I said that to him and he said he would give me a callback.

The next day I did my routine and headed home from my last final I'll ever take. I walked out to my car and heard my phone ring. I picked up the phone and said: "What's up Champ?" "You'll be playing the Roundhouse in two months. Enough time to finish your obligations and certification exams, then play this one last show, Sparky." I dropped my phone and then a load into my pants. Holy shit, this is it, folks. I picked it back up.

"They're willing to book me without a record out?"

"I sent them the masters and they liked what—"

"You sent them the fucking masters without my permission, little fuck?" I told you, they do one good thing and expect the hundred other bad things to go away. He tried to defend himself with, "Hey, I'm just doing your friend Jackie a favor here, buddy. Don't get mad at me. This is mostly for her benefit, not yours."

"Oh, yeah? Well, fuck you, Champ. Find someone else." Not five minutes later I get a call from Jackie. "What the hell are you doing?"

"Jackie, he's being a dick and not listening to me."

"Doug, he said you called him the c-word and you never want to work with me again. Is that true?"

Lying sack of shit, wasn't he? "Jackie, I'll work with you until my days are done, I told him to fuck himself because he sent my masters that are not copyrighted out to different people." "Yeah, that sounds like him. Sorry, Doug, I'll make it right."

As I sat outside with Mister Bruce I got another call. "Dougie, baby, still want to do that show?" I deeply exhaled, "Champ, I will do the show on one condition."

"Name it, buddy. We'll add it to your rider."

"No, Champ. It's a contract negotiation. I will only do the show if I never hear from you about being in this business again. I'm doing this show to go out on a high note. If you hear from me, it will be about writing under my alias for Jackie or for someone else. I will not perform or record my own music again. I'm doing my set the way I want to, with people I audition. You have no say or hand in what I do." Champ might as well have put me on silent. "Yeah, we can get that last minute. No problem." So after I re-explained my conditions, three times over, we came to agreeable terms. I would only deal with him for the release of this one EP, this show, and then I would be gone.

Running everything past Mom and Dad went over rocky at the start, but in the end, they realized this was an opportunity I couldn't pass up. To play this theater was a dream come true. The modicum of success I would be achieving was better than I thought I'd ever actually see come to fruition. The only problem is I couldn't talk about it to anyone I met in the future. I couldn't risk my job over it. But I also couldn't turn my back on a lifelong obsession and not be sure I had conquered everything I set out to. So if anyone ever talked about how good Jackie's show was, the mystery opening act would remain that: just a complete mystery, but a badass one at that.

Things started going well with the plans for the show, but the EP release was a nightmare. Champ wanted to release it on Jackie's label, but I wanted to be as anonymous as possible. I didn't want to be put up on billboards, commercials, or anything like that. I just wanted to put it on various streaming services and be done with it. Let people find it and have it as their indie thing that only they knew about. Then over time, have people find each other and let it be something to connect over. Though that stuff sounds well and nice, Champ thought it would be best for him to buy it outright and have all the control over the songs and the masters. To which, I'd rather spit in his morning coffee than give into him.

He saw the ideas about my album art and just said, "No, no, no. That's not the right direction for you."

"Hey, Champ, you don't own any of it, so keep your mouth shut."

"Yes, Dougie, but my artist is associated with you."

"Your artist's biggest hit is because of me so I'm pretty sure my direction is doing just fine. Get fucked." I don't do well with being told what to do. Never have, never will. My idea for the artwork was very simple. There's this picture I have of Tim's studio all full with his gear after we had cleaned it top to bottom. Then a picture of the room the last day we were there; all empty and bare. It showed how I was full of all the spirit of music, and now I'm just not there anymore. Along with it, on the back was going to be an explanation of the EP and who it was for. I thought it was great for the direction of my life and the fact that this was a one-time effort. Obviously, Champ thought of something original: me sitting in a diner with a guitar. Oh wow, breathtaking, isn't it? I told him we don't want to do it, so he sent his print ahead to get EP's made. I saw the test printing while I was in their office discussing what we wanted to do for the show. I crucified him for that and told him that if he made another adjustment without my consent, I'd drag him to the lobby and beat his ass in front of his clients. A month before the show I got a call from Champ: "How would you like your songs on the radio?" Now we're talking, but of course, my rules or nothing.

"I pick what gets played and you're not in the building."

"Done. You have to be in Chicago in three days to be at the station for the interview." Well, road trip time.

FOURTEEN

Sweet Home Chicago

I tell Ang the news about the radio interview and she really is skeptical of the idea at first. We had a talk about pulling out of music and sticking to only writing under my stage name. However here I am moving forward advertising the music. After we talk it over, we agreed that playing one of our songs on the radio is a chance that neither of us would pass up. And after I agreed that we can stop off at the Rock and Roll Hall of Fame in Cleveland, it is all systems go.

From Long Island to Chicago is a 12-hour drive, so this whole conversation happens mere moments after I get off the phone with dickhead. Figuring that we leave in a couple of hours after we pack, we can pull off in Ohio, see the rock hall the next morning, finish the drive that evening as we pull into Chicago, get some dinner and sleep, then do the interview the next morning. And aren't I just the best boyfriend in the world to spring this all on her in just five minutes? But as luck rarely so has it with me, everything works out and we are on our way. Anyone else thinks this sounds fishy to you, too? A born skeptic like myself is on pins and needles saying, "This is way too good to be true. Something is bound to happen."

So I'm told by Champ that the radio station is a big-time Chicago station that focuses on an artist for a couple of minutes, asks them a few questions, plays the single, and then I'm out the door. Let's see how much of this is true by the time we arrive there. Well, we are not even off Long Island before Ang has done some research and found out it's not a radio station, it's a podcast. Though they are few and far between, podcasts are usually hours long and play very little of the music. Immediately Ang gets on my case with "I knew he'd lie to you, I don't know why we're doing this, if you keep this up after the show, I'm gone." And she's right, I have jumped the gun again. I trusted someone I shouldn't have trusted. "Ang, if you want me to turn back, I will. But let's just call the podcaster and ask if he'll play the music. If he's not playing the music there's no real reason for me to be there." So she doesn't let me call, she calls for me. What a woman. "Hello, is this the 'Nonsense at Noon' podcast?" I can't hear what the poor guy on the other end of the line was saying. Kind of just sounds like the teachers from Charlie Brown. "Yes, hi, this is Angela Bryson from Panic Under Pressure's management. How are you today? I'm good, thank you. Now, I had heard this is a podcast, not a radio station, correct? No there's nothing wrong with that at all, in fact, we prefer them over many stations. We were just told that it was a radio station so we were under the impression his songs were being played. Can you tell me if you guys do that?"

God damn does she do this in her spare time in secret? Or is she a call girl because I'm...sorry, back to Ang.

"You don't play songs on the show. Yes, I understand." I start to put my blinker on to go to an exit ramp and turn around when she pushes my wheel back to the lane and tells me to keep going. "Now, is there any way you can play the songs and then discuss them on the podcast?" I understand it's not something you do but we have several other artists lined up who we'd like to put on the podcast if that becomes an option, including Jackie Ill. Yes, she's a good friend of ours. Sometimes a little too close." She bashes my knee with the side of her fist giving me a big hint. "The thing is, we're coming a long way for the show and the trip is beneficial to us if the songs were played. You understand, don't you?" There was a long pause until I heard, "Fantastic, we'll be at the studio in two days' time. Would anyone like coffee? Great, we'll bring some. Have a nice day!" She hangs up the phone and says, "The coffee is for in case they want you back."

It doesn't take long for me to utter, "Babe, I know we're pressed for time but I'm so willing to pull over for a quickie. You turned me on so much." She smiles but then it quickly turns to, "That's what happens when you use the people who love you to help you."

"Babe, what do you mean?"

"I understand how Tim dying got you in a daze, but with this Champ guy, you hardly pay attention to me or your parents." Oh boy, here comes the lecture.

"I get that you love this and I get this is all you've ever wanted, but why are you trying so hard for something you're just going to give up and let be the past? Put your efforts toward something you know will last forever and be important to you. Like school or your girlfriend. If this was what you wanted forever then fine, I'd get it, but if it's not what you want, after these obligations you have to let it go."

I say it over once in my head to be sure I don't say something stupid. "I know we both love music the same amount and we love to relate, but this is the one thing I want to accomplish in life, hell, the only thing that I've ever cared about. I just want to make my mark. Even if it's such a small mark it goes largely unnoticed. Haven't you ever wanted something so bad enough and now you're on the cusp of making it a reality?" She sits on her legs and says something that knocks me dead. "Yeah and now I have it, you. I've wanted someone to love and care about me above anything else, and until these opportunities came up you've shown it to me. Have I been showing you the same amount of love?"

"Ang you know you have-"

"Then why am I background noise? I'm right here, right in front of you. Willing to show you all the love you could ever get from entertaining people who will move on from you. Why can't I be enough?"

Goddammit if that didn't make me feel as low as Chris does. "Ang, you're absolutely right. You are enough and you're all I need. I swear on all things art, that after this podcast and the show at the theater, I'm done. I'll walk away. I will only write for others. Not go out on my own, because you're all I want for my own." She puts her hands on mine, kissed my cheek, and we just sit in the moment of love and affection we have for each other. Why bother getting the approval of others when you got it from the only person that matters? It never clicked like that for me before. Now, I'll never forget it.

That all happens as we are leaving New York. After a bunch of twists and turns and tickets to take for pay roads, we get on the expressway and head west, west, and west some more. Now back in the day with Chris, we'd make mix CD's to take in and out of the CD player. Since those days are over, Ang and I pass the aux cord around for our playlists from Spotify that we both already have. Needless to say our taste in music is the same, but bizarre, and jumps around more than House of Pain. We started with some Slipknot since it's our band as a couple, I have already said we're odd. Then we jump to The Beatles, Incubus, John Coltrane, Underoath, and Talib Kweli. After a while, we got to Warren Zevon, mom's favorite. She turns on his song "Keep Me in Your Heart For a While," and then this conversation comes up.

"I'm really excited to see the Rock and Roll Hall of Fame, but I'm also a little pissed off at how many people you'd think are in it, but aren't." "What do you mean?" Ang asks. "Well," I say, "Warren Zevon, a songwriter like no other, at this point of 2019, is not in the Hall. There's a staggering number of people who aren't in it who should be."

"Like who?"

"Well, just off the top of my head, Warren Zevon, John Coltrane, Judas Priest, Iron Maiden, and Motorhead." Ang is drinking water at this time so I have to say, I'm pretty proud to have been able to get her to do a spit take.

"What the actual fuck? The people who helped shape most of what is considered the foundations of modern rock music and songwriting today aren't in? Why the fuck are we going, then?"

She has a valid point, but then again I also want to at least stop by it. "I have an idea, let's go stop by, then stand in front and take a picture of us flipping it off."

"Yeah, let's do that!" Ang is bouncing in her seat like I just told her we can go get ice cream. We are still trekking through Pennsylvania so we have quite a way ahead. On the way we bounce around on our playlists, play car games—to which I lost everyone on purpose in order to be a gentleman—and even attempted to drive with my feet. It is a success up until a state trooper almost pulls me over. Not for driving with my feet but because of the stench coming off them. Kidding of course; on why he pulled me over. My feet are still putrid, mind you.

We pull into Cleveland around five pm so it's only open for another half hour anyway. We pull over and park illegally for only a couple minutes, get out, and had a stranger take a picture of the two of us flipping off the museum. We're so classy I don't know how we do it. Champ has told me because of the mix-up, dinner is on him when we get to Cleveland as long as it isn't too expensive. So I take Ang to the most expensive restaurant in town, order two lobsters, which I ate none of, as a big "fuck you" to Champ, order a bottle of champagne for each of us—and I pour mine down the drain since I'm still sober—and tip the waitress the bill. Don't fuck with me and make my girlfriend have to do your job, bud.

We go to bed and wake up pretty early, and have more or less the same road trip activities all the way into Chicago. It feels pretty cool to see the Chicago city limits sign while Ang blasts

"Sweet Home Chicago" by Eric Clapton. We pull into the hotel, get some lunch, went to some local venue to see some live music, then go to bed, all the while realizing Ang was right, I don't need the audience anymore. I'm grateful for them, but I'm putting on the biggest show of my life being around her.

FIFTEEN

Nonsense at Noon

So the Nonsense at Noon podcast is run by two chuckleheads named Johnny and Ronnie, both of which are music junkies like Ang and me, although, they are both two slacker-stoners who run this podcast out of their home. They live to not work. The fact that this podcast is as successful as it is shocking even to them. They're really my kind of guys, particularly since they weren't happy when Champ called after Ang demanding to know why they listened to her and not him. Their response was perfect to me, "She offered to buy us coffee, brahhh," which have remembered, and have even brought in doughnuts. They were already stoned when we walked in so it was like Ang had walked in holding a piece of God Himself. Made it all the better that she walked in through a cloud of smoke so it was kind of like her finishing a long race emerging the champion.

"Alright, so are you Mr. Panic Under Pressure?" says Ronnie through a mouthful of Boston cream. "That's me, man, just call me Doug when we're off the air." "Informal, I like it." says

Johnny exhaling from his cock-shaped bowl. "Look, man, Johnny's smoking from your manager: a dick." I roar with laughter, goddamn if that hasn't made the trip worth it, I don't know what else will. "So, bro, if you want to be on the podcast you gotta spark up with us." And here lies the dilemma. I haven't smoked weed in four years. I have to start applying for jobs in a couple of weeks, but I have to be on this podcast or else I can get in serious trouble with management. I look over to Ang and we have the same look on our faces. We have a telepathic conference and after several seconds of stares, she shrugs her shoulders and says, "You heard the man, take a load from the dick bowl." Ronnie falls out of his chair laughing so hard. "Yo, I never thought of that. Holy shit, it's like I've been swallowing...hey, does that make me gay now?" Stoned people are really a trip. I spark up and cough until my lungs turn green. Here we go.

They pass the bowl over to Ang, "Mrs. Panic, will you be joining us today?" She didn't even say a word. Just took it, sparked up, and took a bigger hit than I ever have—even in my time of smoking—I really ought to consider how much three months of my salary is.

The boys set up the mics, mix the sound and hit record. "Hello, everyone, and welcome back to Nonsense at Noon. It's your hosts Johnny and Ronnie and we're here with someone all the way from New York." Johnny starts out strong then continues. "They here from New Yahk, prick. Hey, I'm walkin' here!"

"Johnny, he may be walkin' here but, man, he ought to be playing here. I gotta say I love this EP we got from him. He's here in the Nonsense Podsense studio with his Mrs. and better half. We got Panic Under Pressure here. How are you today, sir?"

"I'm doing great, boys, I just walked in off the street from my favorite pizza joint after catchin' a Yankee game. Hey, how ya doin'?"

"Johnny, he gets it!" Ronnie says putting his hands in the air like he has scored a touchdown at the football stadium for either of the New York teams, neither of which are located in New York. "In all seriousness, sir, I love these songs you got for us today, but we're kind of bummed this is the only collection of songs you plan on putting out yourself. Is that true?"

"Yes, sir. I'm afraid it is. Nothing against performing but I'm just more of a writer. I'd rather write songs for others to perform. These are the only songs I felt like I wanted to release myself and showcase my talent. After this, it's peace out for Panic."

"Well if that is true I'm happy to say that you'll put out something I'll probably have in my headphones for the next couple of weeks, if not the rest of the year." My heart is doing backflips.

"Now, Mrs. Panic, how do you feel about him doing only the one-time deal? Would you ever want to see him do more, or is it the right thing for him to do?" Ang picks her leg up and folds her arms. "I think he's truly the best writer I've ever met, but he's an even better person. I'm standing behind whatever decision he makes but I think this is the right idea. Good things should have expiration dates, not dolled out until it starts to suck." Yup, I'm finding this woman a white dress. Ronnie lays back in his chair like he has just had his mind blown. "That is a valid point. It's always annoying when you know the party is ending and there are still people eating chips at the bottom of the bowl. It's like, go home, get out of here."

"I feel personally attacked. Why do I?" Johnny asks in an accusing voice. "Because you always do that, bro. You always end up with the bowl on your face licking the bottom cuz you want all of it."

"Only on the lime-coated chips. That shit is the bomb, bitch. Anyway, we're gonna go track by track on what each song is about and how they came about, but before that, are you happy with the way the record came out?"

"I'm very happy with it, yeah. I love the feel and the flow of it. The production is top-notch to my ears and I can't wait to put it out once all the artwork is together and ready for release."

"Yeah, man, I'm sorry to hear about the producer passing away. What was his name?" I take a deep breath. It's still hard to talk about.

"Tim Fallon, yeah. He was a dear friend of mine. The EP is dedicated to him. We had some great times over the years but making this was just the utmost peak of our creative integrity together and making music without him seems kind of weird. The last song is about the incident. Hit by a 90-year-old man with dementia while Tim was on his motorcycle." Johnny choked on his dick bowl.

"What the fuck man. That just killed my vibe."

"Crap, I'm sorry, haha. No, it's obviously sad but I'm just

happy for the time I had with him. We found out a lot about ourselves writing and producing together so to finish it in his honor just seemed like the right thing to do."

"Johnny, I'm tearing up at this shit. Start playing the songs, goddammit."

"Boys, I swear to God I'm not this depressing off the air! Just saying the truth."

Johnny looks at me and says, "Never apologize for the truth, brother. Respect, man, respect."

They pull up a playlist with all four songs on it. Seeing it up on their monitor was pretty cool. The songs that were just ideas in my head are now talking points for us to fuck around with and deconstruct. Life is good. They start with "It's All Over." They hit play and it runs for the whole 3:43. "Boy, did that one sound like you were anxious."

"Haha, a little bit, man."

"Ronnie hasn't been that anxious since he earned his nickname 'leaky dick'."

"Fuck you, dude. Don't talk about your sister like that." Johnny throws a pillow at him and misses by a country mile. They're podcasters, not athletes. "So how did that song come together? What happened to make that one fall out of your noodle and onto the page."

"Well, to be honest, guys, my noodle is not usually working, but when it does it makes shit like that. That song actually came about the day I met Mrs. Panic. Literally about three hours after I met her on the way home from class it started churning, but really came out when I went down to my basement and started jamming." Ang looked at me with her why-didn't-you-tell-me-that face. "I swear, I met this young lady while at school and she dropped a book on my head. So I guess you can say she made it fall out. Right, babe?" They both laughed like hyenas while Ang was blushing. "It slipped out while I was air-drumming—you know that!"

"Whoa, whoa, a babe who air drums? Do you have a sister?"

"Piss off, Ronnie. That's my Mrs. Panic."

"You right, you right. But what did it end up being about, because it seemed like you were uptight over something"

"I was very uptight, yes, you could say that. I had met the young lady and on the way home I was freaking out about how this girl seemed like she was the one for me, but I was thinking back at all my other failed relationships. Between the month-long shitty relationships, the booty callers, and the ex-fiancee' I was sitting in my car on edge going 'I can't do this.' So I went to the basement, came up with the riff, and thought about why I was freaking out and how I could get over it. I came to the conclusion that I had got to be confident that this would be better, and whoever was in my past would not see the great person I would become and they'd have to eat my dust as I strode far ahead of them."

Ronnie doles out a high five. "That's what it's all about, brother. Put the past behind you and keep on trucking. Rock on, sir. Mrs. P, how do you feel now knowing the song is a reaction to your early connection?"

Through ugly tears she says, "IT FEELS GREAT JUST PLAY THE NEXT SONG!"

"Whoa, yes ma'am." They load up "No Pressure" and play all through the 3:52 run time.

"I have to say I think that one is my favorite," Johnny says sparking up and exhaling into the microphone. "I love the opening and how simple it starts then goes into this fucker of a song."

"Yeah, but what were you drinking to get that fucked up?"

"What wasn't I drinking? That's the real question. This was all about one bad evening where we were at a...um." I have to pick my words carefully so I don't say "work party." "I was at a family party with Mrs. P and I made an ass out of myself. So much so I got sober, actually."

"What did you do to Mrs. P?"

"Ronnie, it's okay, we're fine. But no, he made an ass and a hole out of himself. He got so drunk he was falling, belching, and disrobing all over the place. He was so bad I left him at the hotel the party was at and told him to stay in the room until tomorrow morning."

"Hence why roll me over, I'm not sober and so on and so forth. The part where I'm saying "There is no pressure here just want you to know, these are the stories that I've been told," was me hearing how much of an asshole I was the next day. I had to calm down after I recounted my shenanigans and got a hold of myself. It's a song I wanted the message to be right with, but at the same time have something instrumental that sounded interesting. Not just four chords, but do something funky with the pedals. So I used a loop pedal and just overdubbed everything."

"Overdub is what we call my fat sister after she passes out from edibles." "He ain't lying, guys. John's sister eats edibles like they're....like edible." Goddamn, these guys are fucked up.

Next, they cued up "Oh Brother," Chris's song with a 2:40 run time. "Before we play this song, Johnny, this is the one that made you cry."

"Holy shit! You cried at my song, man? I'm honored!" Ang rubs his arms with sarcastic support. "Does Johnny want to cry some more?" Johnny actually wipes tears from his eyes and says "I love my brother too, man, why are we all crying on this podcast what the fuck."

"Hey, only half of us half, sir. You and Mrs. P. stick to yourselves while us men go chop down trees and make fire from scratch. But, yeah, man obviously with this song you love your brother, but was there something that sparked this song? Like did something happen or was it just built-up feelings you needed to get out?"

"I wrote this after my brother and I had a pseudo-argument about how lucky the other one is in comparison to the other. We both apologized mere moments after it happened, but it did start as an argument. I still live at home with my parents working on life and he's a full-licensed doctor in an emergency room out on Long Island."

"Yeah, I already feel like shit compared to your brother."

"Nah man, he'd be flat-out be jealous of you guys. You make money doing something you love. By smoking weed and talking a blue streak about pussy and music no less. He's dealing with the worst kind of shit you can see. And he has to do it with a smile on his face."

"Hold the phone, dude. Ronnie. I never tell you enough how much I love you and appreciate what you've helped me do here, man. I love you for it." Ronnie starts to sniffle and hold back a tear.

"Got you, bitch!," yells not Johnny, but my own girlfriend. The woman is nuts, folks, chocolate-coated and nuts. "Are you two finished enough to let me finish?" Ronnie sniffles back but gives a hand gesture that I take as meaning "go for it."

"So, he always has to be in the absolute worst kind of humanity at all times with no sign of it ever getting better. He works his ass off making sure other people get fixed, and then there are people screaming at him that he's not doing enough. Like that shit always bothers me. This guy worked his bones to the dust to get to where he is. When he was an undergrad, he worked two jobs to be sure he, and the family, were getting by, all the while studying to take the MCATS—the test you take to get into medical school. After he got in, with damn near top marks, he went to medical school and took every opportunity to get better at his craft. If he was up 16 hours a day, he was studying at least eight of them. Stopping only for food, bathroom, or to go to class. He got the residency he wanted, too. A dual residency, meaning he does internal medicine and emergency medicine at the same time, all the while managing a girlfriend and being blinded by student loan debt. The world gave him no quarter, and he asked for no quarter. The least someone could do is write a song telling him "I'll handle our parents, I got it from here, all your hard work will pay off in time."

"Can you all please hold yourselves together?" As the entire room is sobbing at the thought of "I love my brother, here's his song."

They finally hit "play" on the fucking song and it runs out with no interruptions, but we stall going into the next one so everyone can dab their eyes with tissues and blow their nose. Maybe I'm all cried out from Tim, but, common people it's not a movie about a dog. Suck it up.

"Hoooo, I haven't cried that much since I watched Brian's Song." "I don't want to hear it, nah-nah-nah'" I say putting my fingers in my ears. The two jackasses smirked.

"Oh, you don't like Brian's Song do you?" My hands are now covering my ears. "I'm not listening." But of course, these two pull up the end of the flick, the ultimate guy-cry experience. When Billy D. Williams's character says, "I'd like to say a few words about a friend of mine named Brian Piccolo." My head falls into my knees as these fucks start chanting, "Cry! cry! cry!" When the scene ends with "I'd like all of you to love him, too," poor Ang is sitting there watching, saying "I've never seen this and now I never will turn it off!" At least they listen to her.

"Now obviously we touched on the last song a little bit already, and going from that movie to this is kind of fucked-up, but let's dive deep on this. You told us about the circum-stances surrounding his death, but when it comes to your Brian Piccolo, Tim, is there anything you'd like to say before we start the last song?" Now I am going to start crying. "In all honesty, if I had anything else to say it would just be 'I love you, buddy, thank you for helping me find my voice.' Play the song, please."

He cues it up with the run time of 3:29 and let it run. It finishes and respectfully the boys raised these shot glasses full of God knows what, and say, "Rest in peace, Tim Fallon, you did good." They slam them down the hatch, put them upside down, and flicker their faces. Not big drinkers, I see. We keep talking on the podcast for another two hours after that. We talk about shitty movies, a smidge of politics, and what we could do to clone Ang.

"Now, before we get you two out of here, we got to mention this show you have coming up at the Roundhouse in Long Island." I hold up my hand, "First I got to say thank you for having us, gentleman, I know we've taken up plenty of your time, but you're class acts and I appreciate you both." Ronnie gives me a big hug and says into my microphone, you two can come back anytime, podcast or not. Just don't bring that lick bag of a manager."

"Oh! Sick burn, Ron. But yes, Panic Under Pressure will be opening up for Jackie Ill at the Roundhouse Theater on Long Island. On, in, which is it? You being locals and all. We both say "on" at the same time. Goddamn, it's frustrating when people get it wrong. "Sorry, but yes, buy tickets to the Round-house on Long Island to see this awesome show with a lineup of more to come." Every time someone mentioned Round-house Theater, Ang gave them a swift roundhouse kick as a sort of punctuation mark. "This is the Nonsense at Noon podcast and as always I'm Johnny." He gestures to Ron. "I'm Ronnie." Johnny continues, "Keep your Nonsense Podsense with you at all times and remember, don't Panic Under Pressure."

They lower the faders and stay silent for five minutes. I have no idea talking so much would be so draining. Afterward, we decide not to go out to dinner, but to hang out with the boys at their house, get in their hot tub, order some pizzas and have a chill night. We get an Uber back to the hotel later and after we have taken our showers and lain in bed, we are burnt the fuck out, man. We are as crispy as a mother fucker. Nevertheless, my good lady gave me a kiss goodnight and said: "I'm glad we came."

"Really?" I say, knowing she means every word.

"Yeah, it was fun playing hooky from responsibility for a while." We both rolled over and started to fall asleep. Mission accomplished. All that's left is my crippling anxiety about whether this is the right move or not. But hey, don't panic under pressure.

SIXTEEN

Meet the Band

We wake up the next morning and life couldn't be better. I am in Chicago, one of the most important cities in the country for art and culture, with the girl of my dreams, who I love more and more each day, with a job in education. I love my life. I really do. I roll over and give Ang a kiss on the forehead, smell her nasty morning breath that I've grown to love, get up and hop in the shower. I can't help but notice though, in the shower with me is a tight grip around my waist. It's hugging me and giving me kisses on my back. Could it be? But it is! It's Ang coming in the shower with me. Hold on, I have to do something quickly.

Sorry, she had this itch she needed to be scratched. She hops out and goes back to sleep so I go down for some coffee and breakfast from the buffet to bring back to the room. On the way out from the buffet, I couldn't help but overhear the hotel clerk's phone playing the podcast. The boys must have done only quick edits and put it up overnight. Now realizing it's 12:15 and they put it up at noon. Goddamn, I sound funny, and the songs sound great. Can I keep this high forever?

We get dressed, get our bags and go downstairs. On the way out I can't help but tell the hotel clerk, "Hey, you know those guests on Nonsense at Noon? That's me and my girlfriend." He must be a huge fan because he has glassy eyes and starts tearing up saying, "That shit was awesome, yo." I guess the fans of the boys live similar lives. The ride home was more of the same—us being our goofy selves. Until Ang says, "Are you sure it's a good idea to back out of this music thing?" I mean it to be bad because I am thinking the same thing. "Ang I don't know anymore. Yesterday was so much fun, wasn't it?"

"Doug, imagine a life lived like that. Just living in the moment and having fun with people doing nothing but being silly. I know we're really good at our jobs, but this could be a career that makes us happy. You doing your thing and me being there by your side to help if you need it."

"Ang, I'd be there for you too. This is a partnership, not my enterprise." She gave me a big kiss for that. "Good, you've been listening. But in all seriousness, now I see why you chase this life. It's so much fun." I keep my eyes straight ahead after that. "How about we take a week and think about it."

We don't stop off in Ohio this time. We drive straight through, so we get home around one o'clock in the morning. I pull into the driveway to see Mom jumping up and down and Bruce wagging his tail. We get out and give her a hug. "Did you hear the podcast?" She looks at me with confusion then realized what I meant.

"No, sweetheart. I don't know what a podcast is. I checked your student portal and you aced everything. You're a certified teacher!" I felt elated. Far more elated than I ever felt in my life. Ang jumps on me and gave me a big hug. She runs inside and checks her online portal and sure enough, she has aced everything too. We are a teacher and a nurse. The whole world is in front of us on two fronts. And now, the sudden panic sets in. Mom lets Ang stay the night because she knows we have a lot to discuss the next morning and doesn't want to waste any time.

We wake up to sheer horror as I have a sore back and she is cranky pre-coffee. We go out to the porch and talk about everything. We know we want each other, but what do we do to support ourselves? The decision becomes much clearer after I get this voicemail: "Hey, Doug, it's Champ. Give me a call about paying for the trip." I am red from anger. I call him in my usual way. "What the fuck do you mean - pay for the trip?"

"Hey, Doug, good to hear from you. Well, you see, the trip wasn't free. You have to pay for the room, business support, and the bill from any use of the credit card I gave you."

"You told me it was on you, shrimp dick!"

"Well, for the moment it was, but then you have to pay me back. This music business costs money, Doug. I don't know if anyone ever told you that."

"Why the fuck would you offer to pay if it would just be on my dime, anyway?"

"Well, we didn't want to have you worry at the time. The total bill for the trip is about $2485.89 but we can put it on a payment plan if you want." The phone slips out of my hand but Ang catches it. She strokes my arm with a face of "Let me handle it." I let her do it.

After quite an argument, she comes back and says, "Because you're not signing with the label you're going to have to pay it. They also said that since you don't have that money, they're just going to take it from your pay from the show. Which was only about $500.00 so we'll still owe a little under $2000. Baby, I'm so sorry. If I knew—"

I'd never take this out on Ang; I'm just going to have to pay it. Whatever it takes, I'm never going to sign with him. I've dealt with some annoying-ass students, but if I had to work in an industry full of people like Champ, who leave out the truth just to make a profit on your back, then I'll be happy to never go into this business. Jesus, I need a drink. I'm not going to, relax.

"Ang, we'll pay it off. I have the money in my savings. It's not a big deal." She gives me a stink face and says, "Where the hell do you have money between going out and the money you make now?" I guess I have to spill the beans here. I returned Annie's engagement ring and got half the money back. I was saving up to buy Ang one, but I guess that'll have to wait. It's only been just shy of six months, but I know I have found my best friend for life. After I tell her, she drops to the floor in tears, so, I consoled her, and tried to comfort her.

"Honey, it's fine. It's just money. I'll make more." "It's not that, I'm just so happy you started saving up for one. I love you so much." I thought yesterday was a good morning. This one, I'll always remember.

Later in the day, Ang goes home to rest and celebrate her passing with her parents so I have some time to get my act together with putting out applications and making a few calls. As luck has it, I get a call from Max, the principal of my school. I let it go to voicemail because I have no desire to talk to anyone today. "Hey, man, congratulations on passing. I'm pushing your application through for next year. We'll figure out your subject closer to that time, but you have a job. Welcome to the big leagues." Jesus Christ, life is good.

As that message ends, I get a text from Jackie. "Hey, sorry about Champ. He's a dick, but business is business. Let me know if I can help." I shoot her a text back.

"Yeah, he's a dick, but I get it. I wish he'd been upfront about it because I wouldn't have gone at all. Guess that's what you have to do to keep the product going." She responded with, "Yeah it sucks to suck. But look on the bright side, tomorrow you're auditioning players for the live show!" Someone needs to fucking call me with this shit. "Is this your way of giving me a heads up?"

"I guess so. They said they shot you an email."

"Jackie, they don't have my email. I refused to give it to them."

"Well, be at the business office tomorrow. There's a studio in the basement for you to audition and interview the players. Want me to be there?" Though I'd really love her to, I think Ang might cut my throat if I did.

"Nah, I'm good. Thanks though, bud." I let Ang know of course. I get a bone for good behavior. And I'm not talking about Bruce's bones if you know what I—moving on, sorry.

I pull up to the studio, take out two guitars, the pedalboard and amp, and a dolly to move it all with. I bungee cord them to it and head in. Ang follows behind me on her phone, taking pictures since she's never been to anything like this before. "It's like going to camp!" At least she's excited. I've never been more nervous. These aren't my guys. I've played with Tim for the last five years, what if none of them click? Well, only one way to find out. I set up and plugin like I've done a thousand times. It might actually be a thousand times come to think of it. And I wait for the first guy. Here goes nothing.

We cut the auditions into three days. Day one drummers, day two bass, day three lead guitar. Each person brings in their own stuff except the drummers. For drums, we have all the hardware like bass drums, floor toms, but they bring in their own cymbals and snare drum. They have all been given a copy of the EP to learn the songs along with a couple of covers they think would sound pretty cool, if I do. They chose "Simple Man" by Lynard Skynard, "45" by Shinedown, "Use Some-body" by Kings of Leon and "Show Me How to Live" by Audioslave. I can sing loud as a mother fucker. We start out with the originals and then move into the covers. The first drummer comes in and is nice enough, but every time he gets into it, he keeps jumping up too high and missing his crash cymbal. It's kind of important to stay in time and, you know, hit things as a drummer. The second guy is pretty good but has not practiced the covers. So half the songs he doesn't know. Great. The third dude comes in and tears it up, though. He doesn't really speak so I am interested in what'll happen in the interview.

We sit down to talk, and after I say, "Hey, man, you tore it up. Sweet job," he cracks his fingers, twists his neck, spits on the floor and says "Alright, so who's paying me?"

"Excuse me?"

"Listen, man, I know I played the songs better than anyone else who came in so let me tell you how this works. I get paid upfront with no hassle or I don't play. I know this is just one gig and is fun and games to you, but this is my trade and stock, okay? I'm a professional and this is my job. So unless you have anything else for me I'll be seeing you." He gets up and leaves behind the drums for someone from his little entourage to clean up. I don't get up from my chair because I'm in shock to think that anyone would speak to another person like that. Ang, however, almost breaks the door down in the control room to beat his fucking ass. That lovely lad is Jason, and is my drummer for hire for one show, if he survives my girlfriend.

Day two: bass players. The lovely Jason returns to help with the auditions, holstered only by the promise of a hundred dollars and coffee brought to him every time his cup is empty. Bass players can be a tricky lot. I've noticed bass players can be really good, or flat out suck. Players one, three, four, five, and six are really great players. Two and seven are atrocious. Two decides to dress up like he belongs on the sunset strip in the eighties and only plays the root note of what I am playing instead of the real bass parts. Seven outright doesn't know how to play without spinning and losing his chord. We found the ace in the hole in Maggie, player number eight. She knows all her parts, but is really fun and bubbly to be around. All smiles and positivity. She interviews really well, too. After we put our instruments down, she starts in on her pitch.

"Okay, so what do I have to do to be sure this isn't the only EP you put out?" I started giggling, "I'm sorry, dear. This is a one-time thing."

"It's really fun to play, though! It's simple but the parts to be played are the perfect fit. The bass is like Goldilocks, not too much, not too little, but just right."

"Well thank you, Maggie. I appreciate it. Mind if I ask your experience level?"

"I've played bass for about five years and I play in a cover band called Speakeasy. We play at a lot of cosplay events and last year we played Comic-con." I'm impressed, I didn't even know live music was at Comic-con.

"Where at the con did you play?"

"Oh, well, if there's the center of Comic-con, we were nowhere near it. We were in a bar about ten blocks down but a couple of cosplayers and even an actor came down to see us play!" I love a self-deprecating sense of humor. "Do you know which actor saw you play?"

"Yes, he said his name was Nathan. He acted like he liked the band then grabbed my ass after stealing our EP."

"Oh, Jesus Christ. Maggie, that's awful." She shrugged and said, "Yeah, but the worst part was he never called me back." Holy crap, she's funny. I got a death stare from Ang for laughing too hard.

"Do you have any trouble playing the songs?"

"No, not at all, I'm ready to go on stage now if we have the time. Put me in coach, I can do it!" I think I found my new best friend. "Well, Maggie, you got the gig, please be back here tomorrow. We'll be auditioning lead guitar players." She let out a squeal that reminds me of an anime character. I can't remember which one, but I'm pretty sure tentacles were involved.

If you think bass players are a tricky lot, they've got nothing on lead guitarists. We had to go an extra two days auditioning about 20. Everyone has their own style, sound, or take on how the song should be played. All are either fine, good, or "head and shoulders above" professionals. We end up taking a break and go across the street to grab a cup of coffee and some fresh air. While there, we find this dude on the sidewalk playing with his case open. I throw a couple of bucks in before I get my coffee. While in line I can't help but admire the fact that the dude doesn't need a venue to play. He just plays because he loves it. That's how it ought to be done. I end up chatting with him outside for a bit before heading back across the street. "Hey, bro, my name's Doug. You sound excellent." He lets his guitar rest behind his back like he is Johnny Cash. "Hey, man, I saw you guys been coming across the street for a couple of days. You in a band or something?" He shakes my hand by covering it with his other hand. You don't see that kind of kindness anymore. "Yeah, man, I'm playing this one show opening for Jackie Ill at the Round-house and I'm trying to get a band together."

"I don't know who Jackie Ill is, but if you're playing that barn you gotta know what you're doing. God bless, brother." It was like talking to a young Bruce Springsteen, what a down-to-earth guy.

"Hey if you're not still playing, want to come across the street and hear the record I'm putting out?" He got his money together, put his guitar away and picked up the road case like he was trying to catch a train in a hurry. He must have been doing this for a long time.

"Let's roll, bro." We head across the street and before we even play him the songs, we get to talking about life. Turns out his name is Nick. He's from Brooklyn and moved out here to live with his aunt and get away from the craziness out there while he regroups and finds the sound he's been looking for. We play him the tracks and in his own words, he yells, "Alright. I found the sound, man." It breaks my heart to tell him this is a one time deal, but he replays all the tracks just so he can audition. We let him borrow one of the old electrics with a Line 6 amp that we put on the pre-set distortion. He plays those songs like he wrote them himself. God damn, I think I just found another guy I should have been writing music with all along. It's crazy how you can find people you're meant to be around. I'm not sure in anything about God or the afterlife, but I do believe people gravitate toward certain personalities. Which is exactly how I think you're supposed to find lead guitar players. You don't go with the outright most talented, you go with the one who is picking up the vibe you are putting out and gets the direction you want to go in.

Spoiler alert, I don't continue with music. Ang and I get married, stay kid-less, and we just do our jobs while writing music for Jackie and Nick until they feel like stopping. Nick is even my best man. I knew he'd be my inevitable best friend when we told him he got the gig. We tell him as such and he puts his hand out and says "I don't want money, I just want to play. Donate the money to a charity of your choice." Ang gives him the biggest hug I've ever seen. Bigger than any she's given me. I'd feel jealous but I give him one just as big.

So my band is together, I'm playing the Roundhouse Theater in a month, and I have a career in teaching ahead of me to look forward to. Cue the shit hitting the fan.

SEVENTEEN

The Aforementioned Shit Hitting the Fan

S o I have a band, a show lined up, and a list of songs that need to sound even better live than they do on the record. I have a month to get it perfect. Nothing I haven't done before. Though it has been a while, the ambition I usually keep hidden is in full swing. Time to get to work. So each song has the parts that each member will be playing, but there are also a number of parts that we made with either a piano or a synthesizer used on a computer program. Since there's not a lot of time left, we decide it would be better just to have any parts with keys to be pre-programmed and timed to the show to be played through the PA system. All we need is one person to hit play when the cues come up. Simple right? Guess again. That's just one delegation for one person.

On any crew of people working on a set, there is always a crew manager and stage manager along with all the workers making the show run smoothly. Everyone has their job and it is not to be interrupted unless there is an emergency. Though it sounds serious, some of it can be absolutely silly. "Hey dude, you're supposed to be pulling the curtain."

"Fight me, bro. I gotta put out the stage props."

"Tough shit, Noodles is gonna do it, you gotta do the curtain, then help do the third costume change." None of my stage shows are anything close to that, but some can be.

Cut to the week before the show, we have two people helping the entire production: one to run errands in case anyone needs anything, and one to do sound. That's not including what needs to be done as far as lights, instrument techs, stage management, striking crews to change bands one after another, and the runner to do errands. Forget one person to do the keyboard sounds, we need an overhaul of people to get this shit done. And since Champ's so lovely, it has all been delegated to me since he has finally had enough and said, "You wanted this show so bad, you set it up. You ain't paying me." It sounds like a curse, more like a gift. My show, my way.

Before anything gets done to get this show set up, let me tell you about everything that has gone wrong in one day and that almost got everything canceled.

We were posting the job on a social media site that advertises for stagehands. In return, they get beer or entrance to the show for free. All of a sudden I get a phone call from Champ. "Champ, to what do I owe the displeasure?"

"Just wanted to let you know you're being sued for copyright infringement." Cue armpit sweat and a migraine.

"What the hell? Who's suing me and for what reason?"

"You're being sued by a band in Chicago over the song 'It's All Over' and it's over the entirety of the song. They say it's far too similar to one of their songs called 'Over and Out.'" I have never heard of this band or the song so how can this be? The dick sends me the song and I have to say, it makes me nervous. The structure is similar, the lyrics run the same way, with a similar message, and even the guitar solo sounds the same. This is bad, really bad. I called the lawyer for the management company to call the band and ask certain questions. If my phone call was at 10:00 in the morning, the phone call that would save my ass comes at 4:45 in the evening. Fifteen minutes before he closed up for the day.

"Doug, you're all in the clear."

"What the hell happened?"

"Well, you can blame Champ because he called the band about the song and thought they'd want to hire someone to pursue a suit against you so he can get some money as a finder's fee. The band wasn't interested in suing you. Even if they were, they didn't have their song copyrighted so, if anything, they just found out that they're the ones in an actionable position. Not you."

"Can anyone go to Champs office and beat his ass into the ground, please?"

"You only have to deal with him for another week. Let it go." I thank him and even pay him a small amount of money for having my back. Anything Champ can do to get extra money he'll fucking do.

Next, I get a text from Max. "So what's this about Panic Under Pressure, hmm?" My heart almost falls out of my chest. I play dumb. "I thought I just wasn't allowed to use my real name. Not just cut music out like a tumor."

"Well, Doug, you're my tumor. One of the students was playing a song from your record in the cafeteria the other day. I've been hearing you play and write since middle school so I know your voice when I hear it. What were you thinking?"

"I was thinking I could do something under a different moniker." I saw the three little bubbles come up and disappear God knows how many times. After a while, it resulted in this. "Look, the school board doesn't know. I only know because I got you to confess it through here. So I guess it'll be our little secret. Tell me you aren't playing a show at the Roundhouse, though."

My response was, "I heard that band Panic Under Pressure is opening for Jackie Ill, you want to go with me?"

"Goddammit, Doug . . . sure I'll go, but you need a disguise to have plausible deniability and you don't know me. You don't speak to me. Got it?"

"You got it, boss."

After I have almost lost my song, money, and career all in the span of one afternoon, I decided to change my underwear after almost shitting myself enough times today. That is until I get a message from Jackie. "Hey, how quick can you learn a song?"

"Depends. How hard are we talking?"

"All four-chord songs."

"Jackie, you said a song. What's wrong?"

"So my guitar player quit and I'm playing for an hour and a half. So I need you to learn twenty songs by Friday night." So I change my underwear again and realize these last-minute deals with music will give me a peptic ulcer sooner than I want. Jackie sends me the list and though they aren't hard, it's a fucker of a setlist to learn in a week. So I get put on a schedule of practicing every day with my band, then stay for an extra four hours to rehearse with Jackie. I can't wait for this to be over.

So if all this happened on a Monday, Tuesday through Friday were by far some of the most exhausting times of practice I've ever done. I play for about 45 minutes, then Jackie gets her hour and a half. Every day we go to practice, Ang has to drive me since I am so tired and stressed out. And all that week if it isn't one thing, it's another. Every day there is a new problem.

Although I love two-thirds of my band, God damn, they can be frustrating. One day Maggie forgets her music, then spends an hour running home getting her music and then an extra 45 minutes getting food. By the way, catering was brought to practices. A gift from Jackie no less. Another day Nick forgot his capo. A song that requires a capo is already a song that needs special attention. The strings have to be put on properly and sometimes they break, Sometimes an open string with a capo can be nowhere near where you're supposed to be on the fretboard. So when Nick forgot his, the two songs that needed it sounded like absolute garbage. And if that wasn't enough Jason was, well Jason.

Every day before he started playing he'd hand me a newly edited version of his rider. A rider is something a performer needs—or in his case demands—in their dressing room or on stage to be done, or else they cannot perform. Mine is the shortest by far. Bottled water and wet wipes. Maggie asks for water, chips and guac, and adequate WiFi so she can be on her phone. Nick asks only for peace and quiet for meditation. Yes, his is cheaper, but peace and quiet backstage is damn near impossible. Jason demands at all times to have his coffee-filled, a massage station with a masseuse, the furniture to match whatever wall decorations, catering for his entourage, his entourage to have matching jackets for the gig, and for him to have full access and be able to make changes and final say to the setlist. I am willing to give him a cup of coffee from across the street. I'm not paying for any of this and neither is Champ. Every day it was given to the stage managers we hired from off the street and every day we find it in the trash. This is all going to backfire unless something is done.

So on Thursday, he comes in with his newly revised rider, and his new inclusion is to have sunflower seeds peeled and fed to him on the couch while he wears a robe. Not already de-seeded seeds, but seeds in the case, to be peeled in front of him by the lead singer's girlfriend. Oh boy, where do I start?

I don't know where this little shit has the nerve to demand these things. The nerve to be fed things like Cleopatra on a couch, let alone by my girlfriend in this absurd power move. Nevertheless, I did nothing but laugh. I showed it to the entire band and crew before showing Ang. She saw it, took a deep breath and jumped behind the kit punching the shit out of him and cursing his ass out. "You little mother fucker, who do you think you are, you misogynistic little shit, I can't wait to see you die alone." Oh my God, I couldn't breathe I was laughing so hard. He tried to get up and quit but Nick stood over him, making him cower in fear, and said "you're doing this show if you want to keep your legs. And now you're doing it for free." He sat his ass behind the kit and didn't say a word until he stepped off stage on Friday, the nasty little shit.

EIGHTEEN

How to Put on a Show

Now I have briefly talked about the low amount of staff we had available for the show, but let me tell you what it really takes to put on a show. Not in metaphors or fancy pseudo-intellectual descriptions, but what it takes financially, in manpower, and the mental toll it takes on someone.

So let's start with the venue. Whether it's a club, theater, Coliseum, or even an American Legion Hall, there is always a flat fee to rent the space to play. Each place will vary and the bigger you go, the bigger the cost. In our case, the Roundhouse Theater costs us just shy of $10,000 dollars. So if you're playing a theater, you better be sure people are coming and that ticket prices are set to the appropriate level. Since Jackie is the biggest act on the bill, and not even really that big, tickets are being sold for $75 dollars. We, therefore have to sell 200 tickets just to break even before other expenses are even mentioned—already hard enough when we're relatively unknown. So that's why we're booking other acts besides the two of us to be sure the other bands can bring people in. Though I'm opening for Jackie, opening for me is that band Arrowhead from Chicago who Champ almost tried to get to sue me. Since I had the upper hand, as an apology I got them booked to be my opener. Opening for them are two other bands. Rattattack from Long Island, and Sleeper Agent from Fairfield, Connecticut. The three opening bands are given 20 tickets each to sell in pre-sale. You can either sell them to people or just fork out money and give them away. Unfortunately, pay to play is the only way that places are guaranteed to get their money back before people start ordering food and drinks. I have to sell 40, and Jackie has 100. Her being the headliner, all eyes are really on her. The amount of responsibility can really get you sweating. The financial burden alone is ungodly.

So after the venue is booked, it's up to the promoter to get the show heard about and to put asses in seats. Promoters usually take a fee of anywhere from 3-10% of the ticket cost which is why they usually set the ticket price. The one at the Roundhouse takes a fee of 5%, therefore taking in revenue of $3.75 per ticket. If the show sells the 200 ticket minimum, he makes $750 dollars. They have to spend a lot of money on advertising, too. For instance, to promote on a local FM radio station, it costs $2,000 upfront for spots to be run for the month. We only have about two weeks of promotion so they knock it down to $750. That's basically him giving his paycheck for someone to talk for two weeks about a show that few people even care to go to. So they make every artist on the bill post to their social media about the event and damn near barrage us to be on top of it. Though the venue holds 2000 people, it's highly unlikely a local band is going to sell out this place. I thought I'd be nervous playing guitar, I'd be losing hair by the fistful if I had that poor sap's job.

Now the road crew we mentioned: but they rarely, if ever, get paid for small-time shows. Usually, the roadies are parents of the band or reluctant best friends who are paid by free admission to the show. As a joke sometimes they may be paid with fast food. The people we got from the site are pretty good though and are dictated to by Dad and Chris, making sure everything is set because I'm such a bundle of joy. Not.

House lights and sound guys are usually paid a flat rate fee by the venue, but oddly enough, a lot of bands bring their own PA systems and pay them themselves to lower ticket prices so it's easier to get people to come. Sometimes they can be expensive, and sometimes you get someone who just wants to be on the road and will volunteer to do it just because they love doing it. Those are my favorites, those who work well, and are cheap.

And if you have bands or artists coming from out of town, costs can start piling up in terms of hospitality. Think hotel rooms, busses to take them from gig to gig, amenities for people who're high maintenance like Jason. Now obviously where they stay, the number of people, and how diva-like they are is taken case by case. But even the most conservative number can run up to about $500-$1000 bucks a night.

This all comes before artists get paid. Some get about $50 dollars each, some get $50 for the whole band. Some get absolutely nothing. But if you have a good manager—as I don't—the more you play and the more your reputation develops, the higher you get paid. And that's how people like the Coliseum players get paid hundreds of thousands of dollars for, at max, four hours of work.

What I'm trying to say is, touring and doing these shows is expensive as hell. The amount of pressure, and how deep under the microscope you're analyzed, is immense. Obviously, it isn't open-heart surgery to call a phone and fork over the money, but the balls it takes for an artist to walk into a venue, do what they do best, know it was a total success, and not have it be an absolute financial disaster, takes a set of cajones. When I find mine, I'll let you know. I'll be in my classroom with absolute ignorance on what it takes to keep a school running. Just show up with my cup of coffee, shut up, and teach.

NINETEEN

You Better Have Show Etiquette

When I was 15, Dad took me to my first open mic at a coffee show in town. I had what I was going to wear all picked out, my set was ready, and my friends and some girls were coming. I had everything ready, or so I thought. What I failed to realize is that every live performance, from coffee houses to Woodstock itself, has show etiquette. I, being bright-eyed and bushy-tailed, got to the place early, and put myself third or fourth. That's not so bad. Other people needed to go first so they could play and go to work or go to another open mic that night. What I failed to do, was to show any form of respect to the people going on before me.

What I did was this. While everyone had their guitars and other instruments in cases lined up on the wall and labeled, I kept mine out and was playing in the corner while the other performers were on stage. I then started making out with a girl in front of the performer, not to mention shouting "Free Bird" at each performer. Just to let you all know, the "Free

Bird" guy at the show, is the most hated guy at the show. I then went up, did my thing, and came off. Dad snatched my guitar out of my hand, threw it in the case, and said "get in the car" through his gritted teeth. I thought it was because I messed up a chord change. I was thinking in my head, "Oh no Daddy, I promise I'll get it right next time." But, oh no, this is way worse than missing that Em7 change.

In the car on the way home, totally leaving my friends behind, I was berated on what I had done wrong and how my behavior was deplorable and embarrassing. "You're not coming back to any one of these until I tell you you're ready. I've never been so disappointed in you." So while all of you get to be spared Dad's wrath, here are some of the basic rules of show etiquette. On and off stage, audience member or performer.

Performing etiquette has its own set of rules. It's like having two sets of crowds. When you're the performer, headliner or opener, you're on display. Your behavior and the way you present yourself at shows are indications of what it's like to work with you. If you're not listening to the rules, nobody's going to want to work with you.

Starting with rule number one, treat the roadies and staff with respect. Everyone is busy and stressed out trying to make your show a success. You're basically their boss. If you don't treat your workers with respect, they won't listen or will outright sabotage you. Thank them, ask how they're doing and if they need any help. Get them some water or beer if they need it. Oh, and to any singers in bands or solo artists, just because you don't play an instrument doesn't mean you get to sit out at load in. Without your brand, you're singing karaoke. Do you know when your band is considering their solo careers the most? When you don't help. Get to work.

Rule number two, unless you're a stand-up comic, or as interesting as the boss, keep your stories on stage short and sweet. Think of it like this, your joke or story better have, at max, six lines total. Three or four of which to set it up, give a punch line, say "This song is about the last girl who broke my heart, sing along if you know it," then play. Nothing is worse than the singer who doesn't know how to get out of a story he's telling. You sing for a reason, you suck at talking.

Rule number three, to follow suit with rule two, if you're not a politically charged act, like Rage Against the Machine, Bill Marr, Louis Black, or Stray From the Path, and you go political, expect to have people boo you or be disinterested in you. Politically charged acts can be badass, don't get me wrong. But if you're notoriety is based around a song you have about a girl, dogs, or a pickup truck and start talking about something else, you're digressing away from what your crowd is there for. Your job is to play what they want or what they're willing to hear. They have jobs too, and if they can be possibly fired from that job by expressing political agendas at work, you should be held to the same standard. Yes, court jesters and minstrels did it back in the Dark Ages, but it's no longer dark, and you're being paid quite handsomely. Play the one about the girl.

Rule number four, if you're done performing, get behind the merchandise table and mingle with the crowd. Or go into the crowd and be an extra body to support the next band. It's cool to see the person you just saw on stage acting like a normal person, mainly because you are normal. Get rid of that barrier of you being better or disengaging and say thank you to the people who bought a ticket to see you perform. Or, get in the crowd and be there for the next act because they were either there for you or they were warming up the crowd doing merchandising, too. And if they were being dicks, show them how it's done. Be the example you want to set out at these shows.

And lastly, no touching the instruments of the other bands. They're set to how they like it. Nobody cares what you want, except your people. I was doing a talent show a couple of months after I was allowed to play live again and as I was in the cafeteria tuning up, away from other people, all of a sudden, I see a buddy of mine pick up the next act's guitar and start de-tuning it from standard tuning to a whole step down. Forget the fact that he has his own that I had already tuned up for him, but he picked up something that doesn't belong to him and changed it mere minutes before someone else had to go on stage. He de-tuned it, played maybe a minute, put it down, then walked away. The guy came out to get his guitar and as he played it, he was so distraught about it, having no time to fix it before going on stage, I came out, explained what happened, loaned him mine, then fixed his so he could use it in his next song. I even brought it out to him on stage. It is so mind-numbingly stupid to think you can touch or change anything you want on someone else's instrument. I told my buddy that if it happened again, I was letting him get the ass-kicking he deserved. As should anyone who does that.

Now, audience members, you're not excused from this conversation. You do some dumb shit, too. So let's go over some basic survival tips and do-goodery you can do at shows.

Rule number one, while there's a performance going on, keep your mouth shut unless it's short, sweet, or funny. Nobody cares about your commentary unless it is on a DVD bonus feature or podcast. Unless it's an emergency, save it for the car. You don't see people talking in a movie theater. And if you do, what do you do? You "shoosh" them. Except you don't shoosh at a show, you politely ask someone "Excuse me. Can you shut the fuck up? Your lack of basic decency seems to be interrupting my enjoyment of the performance. If you cannot shut the fuck up, please leave. Thank you and have a nice day." Actually, that kind of negates my whole point. You know, just say "Shut the fuck up."

Rule number two, have a sense of decency in the mosh pit. We could do a whole chapter on etiquette in the pit, but stick to these things most importantly: Don't drag in people who don't want to be dragged in, if they fall down, pick them up, and no elbows. Back in high school, we had a guy who ignored all these rules. Since he had to be taught a lesson, we let him go in the middle and then we all bum-rushed him. We didn't kill him, we just wanted to have him "maimed or gravely injured." Bless you, Dobby, you're a free elf.

Rule number three, if you have to smoke, just go outside. I don't know why you would do it, anyway. This has been stamped onto everyone's head since grade school, so why should it suddenly become okay at shows? Not everyone wants to breathe in what you're smoking. Weed or otherwise. Go outside. By the way, if you leave and can't go two hours without smoking, you have bigger problems at hand than showing etiquette, my friend. Often enough, if you leave you can't be let back into the venue anyway unless they have a designated patio or door that goes outside. So put the butts away. Unless you're at a rap concert. Get it?

Rule number four, don't hold up the merchandise line. We all know the girl behind it is hot. It's probably a band mate's girlfriend or sister. Just buy your shit and go. No, they don't have changing rooms. If you don't know your own shirt or pants size, you're far more useless than you know.

And lastly, put the phones away. I don't know how else to say it. Forget about the performer being distracted, it's annoying when you stick your phone up and block the views of people who can't see. Or when they stick it in the air and hit tall people straight in the chin. And to those people who like to record a snippet of a song and post it on social media, that's cute for maybe one song, but stop clogging our feeds with your shitty camera angle and bad singing. It's like a big "fuck you" to everyone who watches. If I wanted to see the concert, I'd have bought the tickets myself. There's a reason performers are starting to lock up phones at live venues. You're not responsible enough with it.

Now obviously these are satires and musings of how people should be at shows, but in all honesty, just don't be a dick. It's that simple. If you can't be pleasant, just stay at home.

TWENTY

The Big Night

B efore we go any further, I just wanted to say the show went over without a hitch, it was by far the best experience I ever had with music and I went out on top with a bang. We sold the fucker out and we had the time of our lives. I could've dropped dead after I finished. If it never gets better than that, so be it.

I woke up, and all day I was going through my checklist of what had to be packed and how it had to be loaded up. Ang came over and was re-checking everything I was doing since I was a nervous wreck. Load in time was 3:00 pm, so all morning I was checking my watch saying "Okay another six hours. That's six episodes including commercials of 'Breaking Bad.' Okay, another four to go." I then took a nap and woke in a panic. Have you ever fallen asleep and forgotten what day it is? I do often. It scared me so much I almost started crying because I had thought I had missed the show. Ang told me to get back in bed I have another 2 hours. She woke me up and we headed down. We were the first ones there followed by

Jackie and the other bands. Oh man, did these bands not hear Dad's speech. Besides the fact that they didn't help any of us with load-in, they passed on meeting the owner backstage and went across the street to get some barbecue sandwiches and dollar iced teas. They didn't tip any of the bartenders and they got smashed before 5:00 pm. The doors opened at 7:00, the first band was on at 7:30 pm. If you start late, you don't get that time back. That's just the time that you lost. Sorry, don't be so shitty next time. Although I have to say, those guys sucking made me look ten times more professional and show-cased how decent the band and I were.

The reason I included that part about start time, is because the first band, Sleeper Agent, missed theirs by about 10 minutes. If we give you a half-hour, you just blew a third of your time. They played pretty decently, but they were more about the show than sound. If you were a movie maybe I'd have your back when it comes to sights over sound and dialogue, but come on, man, act like you've played guitar before. They came in dressed looking as if Aerosmith and Johnny Depp had a love child with the number of scarves and bracelets they wore. They walked on with their tallboys and started sniffling and spitting on stage like they were suddenly stricken with a postnasal drip. Fucking gross.

Rattattack was my pick from Long Island. They were an art-house band who, until today, were really nice dudes. They were short and snippy with staff and demanded things for a chorus of people that were supposed to come on stage during one of their songs. Maybe they were nervous, but I didn't care enough to ask, I had my own shit going on. Let them destroy their own reputations. They played three songs, all of which came out fine, but had so many bizarre parts that they made the audience look at each other with confusion. When you're met with polite applause instead of "Woos" and "You rock," something has gone wrong and you need to fix it. But then they had this chorus for their last song. They all came out in these robes that were multi-colored and had the band's symbol on it. They were a three-piece band so after the chorus came out, the singer/guitar player put his instrument down and took a maestro's baton and started conducting the audience. Of about 2000 people, they had their own fan base of about twenty, all of whom knew the words. It looked bizarre and like something that belonged in the Hollywood Bowl. But here it was tonight at a rock concert. Whatever, guys.

Finally, Arrowhead went on. The worst of the bunch. The guys I technically could have sued and got them this gig to show them no hard feelings decided to go on a tirade for five of their 30 minutes about why I sucked and they shouldn't buy my record. Which only drove people to buy my record. I should have sued for slander but they destroyed their own reputation, anyway. They flat out sucked. They invited friends on stage to dance and they'd stop in the middle of a song saying, "Oh I don't remember how that one went." By the way, that was a Metallica song they stopped in the middle of. They were crucified for that and booed off the stage. I would have been embarrassed for myself, but I was smiling ear to ear. I couldn't have had a better intro if I wanted. They were the worst opener I've ever seen in my life. It was a guideline for how to be mediocre.

It was time to go out; it's my turn to make a statement. I had my rules, I had my set, I had a job to do, and I was going to do it well. The lights dimmed down and I had my introduction done by the boys from Nonsense at Noon. They made the crowd crack up and put them in good spirits. After that Arrowhead horror show, they needed it. I got myself together and let the show start the way we rehearsed. Jason went out first and started the drums to "It's All Over." Maggie came out second and they started an eight-bar bass and drum duet. Then Nick came out. Already the crowd was in much better spirits. They were getting palatable music. Nicky comes out and kept one note going palm-muted at one rhythm so Maggie and Jason can keep up the duet if it went well. After that was done, I took a breath and walked out with my hand in the air to say "hi" with a big shit-eating grin on.

The place didn't know who I was, but they knew already I was for real. I kept things light on the mic. "Sorry about that before, that other band gets a little cranky when they haven't gotten their daily spanking." the whole place laughed. "Don't worry. We'll give it to them. I just wanted to say thank you to everyone coming out and for all of you to know it means the world to us." I let them applaud some more. "Make sure you stick around for Jackie Ill, alright?" Let them applaud some more. I reached my line limit so I walked back to Jason, had my ass to the crowd and started playing the riff that started this whole thing. I was shaking my ass in time and having fun. After they had eaten up the song, I knew this show was going to be amazing. We didn't waste time and went straight into "No Pressure." I started the song with the loop pedal so I had the camera zoom in on me while the lights dimmed low. Ang told me after that the moment made her...um...flood her basement? I guess if that's accurate. But the synth matched the timing of the band and it killed.

After that, I took a swig of water and vamped. "We sound alright out there?" The crowd was loud but sounded soft. "I said we sound alright out there?" The crowd got even louder. "Because you sound beautiful up here." I put the water down. "This next song is one of my favorites, hope it's one of yours, too." Then we kicked into "Use Somebody," to this day, one of my favorite songs. That went well, then nobody spoke, but we put our capos on and played "Oh Brother." Chris didn't have a dry eye the whole night, and neither did I, in truth. The whole time I felt like I was on the verge of tears.

"This next one is gonna be a little bit more serious in the message, and on my vocal chords. Regardless, it's Nick's favorite. While you're at it, make some noise for Nicholas Basquiette huh?" The place went nuts for him. He started playing "45" and the crowd went wild. The same thing with "Simple Man," except I had to make the obvious joke, "Maggie, if you play your cards right and listen to the words, you too could be a simple man." We were greeted with applause and a middle finger from Maggie.

After that was done I thought I was going to pass out. Next was "Long Long Gone," the song I wish I hadn't been given the chance to write. I said as much on the mic. "This next song is a tough one, folks. This song was written for the man who recorded this EP and, to be honest, I'd give it up just to have him back for another day. He did all the drums on the EP and I gotta say, he'd have torn this place up." The song started and we were greeted with lighters and cell phones with the flashlight on waving back and forth. I made it through, but barely.

Lastly, I played my favorite song and the one I taught myself to sing to. "Ladies and gentlemen, this is a night none of us will ever forget. Thank you so much for coming. You didn't give me life, but you showed us how to live. Rest in peace. Chris Cornell. Nicky, kick that shit off, will you please?" While Nick started the riff I threw Jackie some love. "Who here is excited for Jackie Ill, huh? The place went ballistic. "Show Me How To Live" is a mother of a song to sing, so after I did that scream at the end, I simply said "You guys are incredible, we're Panic Under Pressure, we love you, good-night," and just dropped the mic on stage. It was badass.

I went to my dressing room to take a shower and change before playing Jackie's set, but Ang was waiting back there in need of me to fix the flood problem. I went back out all sweaty and gross but I played my ass off. We did our duet and Jackie did something that knocked me dead. She said "Ladies and gentlemen, Doug Manning." The place went ballistic chanting "Doug, Doug, Doug!" It was amazing to hear, but I had an even better view. I saw my beautiful girl staring at me with all the praise and honor I couldn't have gotten from 10 of those crowds. I had 2000 people in there, but I was really playing for an audience of one. I know this whole time I've been saying "fuck this business it's good for nothing," but everywhere is like that. I'm not leaving music because I hate it, I'm leaving because I love teaching and being with Angela more. If you want to make it in music, go for it. The road ahead is filled with the traffic of others doing it as well. But if you can figure out the path to get there and do it with earnestness, integrity and, most important of all, legally, then godspeed and good luck. I'll be here, listening.

Made in the USA
Middletown, DE
16 November 2019

78845242R00099